To Shelly!

Enjoy the book!

Shannon
Donovan

Spring's Reign

Holly's Revelation

Shannon Donovan

Bloomington, IN      Milton Keynes, UK

authorHOUSE®

AuthorHouse™
1663 Liberty Drive, Suite 200
Bloomington, IN 47403
www.authorhouse.com
Phone: 1-800-839-8640

AuthorHouse™ UK Ltd.
500 Avebury Boulevard
Central Milton Keynes, MK9 2BE
www.authorhouse.co.uk
Phone: 08001974150

First published by AuthorHouse   1/22/2007

ISBN: 978-1-4259-7757-3 (e)
ISBN: 978-1-4259-7756-6 (sc)

Library of Congress Control Number: 2006911318

Printed in the United States of America
Bloomington, Indiana

This book is printed on acid-free paper.

There is freedom within, there is freedom without.

Try to catch the deluge in a paper cup.

There's a battle ahead, many battles are lost,

But you'll never see the end of the road

While you're traveling with me.
Don't Dream It's Over
Crowded House

Other Books by Shannon Donovan

Winter's Spark: The Saga of Holly Andrews

Table of Contents

From The Vestiges

As Holly watched through her kitchen window a light spring rain was beginning to fall upon the grass in her backyard. The leaves of the many fruit trees that inhabited her yard appeared to immediately turn themselves skyward in anticipation of the heavenly nourishment. Pulling the window in front of her aside, Holly breathed in the scent of the dampened earth as it drank from nature's cup. Several small sparrows began gathering upon a medium-sized stone birdbath that was parked directly in the center of the yard. Holly smiled as she watched them drink and bathe; wildly fluttering their petite wings and singing sweetly. This tranquil and beautiful space filled with all of nature's gifts would soon host Holly and her fiancé Mark's upcoming wedding reception. The two are to be married soon in a simple ceremony downtown. After which they plan to return home to greet their many friends and family and celebrate the blessed union. Holly glanced at her watch, and noticing that it was nine o'clock, placed her coffee cup into the sink and set about to prepare to meet with the event planner; who was due to arrive at the house in less than an hour. There were many loose ends to gather together and Holly hoped that she could get through this day without her past intervening. Several long months had passed since Holly's horrifying ordeal with her ruthless ex-husband Trevor Morgan and the subsequent fire that took his, and his small son's, life. Holly never thought that she would have made it this far with all that she had endured and at the hands of that maniacal man.

Holly struggled daily to keep those terrifying thoughts from getting the better of her and that wicked winter season was one that she would not soon forget.

"Are you gonna be alright going it alone today?" Mark asked as he watched Holly at the kitchen sink, once again fighting to regain her composure. Mark was headed off to work but always made sure before leaving that Holly was not living too long in her head. "Yes, I'm fine. I'm just going over a few questions that I want to ask the event planner. Don't worry." She assured. Holly knew that Mark loved her deeply and was always concerned about how she fared day to day since the incident. "Great." Mark began. "I'll be home around four-thirty and we can go over everything that you found out today." He exclaimed as he walked slowly toward Holly and then gently gathered her into his strong embrace. Holly snuggled up against Mark, wrapping her arms around his waist, and let him hold her for as long as he could. She was safe in his arms and nothing, nor no one, could hurt her there. "Sounds like a plan." Holly agreed as the two parted. She then watched the only man that she had ever truly love, head for the front door to begin his day. After the incident with Trevor, Mark had insisted that Holly move immediately into his house and away from all of the terrible memories that swirled around Holly's apartment. "A fresh start for a fresh year." Mark had commented happily as he loaded the last of Holly's boxes into his truck. He then grabbed Holly's dog Weber by the leash and handed him over to Holly's sister Mileena. Holly would be in no shape to care for the little puppy, and Mark knew that Mileena had a soft place in her heart and would love him just as Holly had.

But fresh starts were not always as easy as one would imagine. Just because you change your scenery, or a particular person no longer exists in your life, doesn't mean that it will erase your recollections entirely. And if your memories were of the type that Holly had experienced, they would intrude much longer. Her sister Mileena was a prime example of that. Since the fire, and Holly moving in with Mark, she had become distant. The normally sociable, upbeat, and "live life like it was your last day" sister that Holly knew and loved was now reserved and seemed to be preoccupied. Holly figured that everyone had their own way of dealing with tragedy and that Mileena would eventually come around and return to her normal self. A rap at the front door brought Holly out of her revelry. Seeing as though it was most likely the event planner Holly made another mental note to call Mileena, once she was finished today, and see how she was doing.

Mileena sat in her office, that overlooked her hair salon *Drake's Designs*, and watched her stylists milling about. They were busy with clients that required shampooing, hair cuts and colors, facials and manicures, and the many other services that Mileena offered to the distinguishing client. She was proud of her accomplishments and had come along way in her career since becoming a hair stylist herself over 15 years ago. Mileena had always dreamed of owning her own shop and she busted her butt to make her dreams a reality. She now owned one of the county's best salons in Oakland County, Michigan. Drake's Designs has been featured in style magazines, cosmetology trade papers, and proudly Mileena now had her very first television commercial that ran twice daily.

Mileena had everything she dreamed of. But she also kept a terrible secret. A secret that could potentially destroy her sister Holly; were she ever to find out about it. This secret weighed heavily on Mileena ever since the day that she received a letter in the mail. And today, once again, she struggled with whether or not to tell Holly. It was a few months after the fire and Mileena, like most days, went out to claim the days mail from her mailbox. As she walked slowly back to her house, shuffling through the many pieces, Mileena's eyes caught one piece in particular. It was a regular white, hand addressed envelope but without a return address indicated anywhere. The postmark was from the adjacent township of Waterford. But what was really strange was that the address read: *"Holly Andrews c/o Mileena Drake."*; Mileena's address following. Never had Mileena received mail at her home for Holly before. Her steps quickened as she entered her home and walked steadily into the dining room where she sat upon the nearest chair and just stared at the strange piece of mail.

Mileena took the envelope and held it up to the large light above the dining room table, but wasn't able to make anything out inside. The sender used a security envelope that wouldn't allow even the brightest of lights to penetrate through. Should she just hang on to this letter until she saw Holly, or open it first and shield Holly from it's contents? The obvious would be to give it to who it was intended for. But due to Mileena and Holly's past, and also because she had the strangest feeling that this was not any normal letter, Mileena took it upon herself to open the envelope.

Mileena hastily unfolded the single sheet of paper from inside and began to read.

Her eyes widened with alarm as she took in all that was presented to her and in glaringly large letters. Mileena quickly refolded the piece of paper, letting the horrendous warning to her sister sink in. "My God." She began with a feeling of impending horror. "I thought Holly would be safe by now." She whispered aloud. "I thought that between Mark and myself that my sister could now finally begin to heal." Then very quickly a thought occurred to Mileena and reason kicked in like lightning. "If this letter was sent here, and in care of me, than the sender doesn't have a clue as to where Holly lives now." Mileena rationalized growing excited with the fact that she could quite possibly spare her sister this news. But how did the sender know where Mileena lived? That question wasn't too far fetched. Mileena Drake was well known in the county, and for that matter several surrounding counties. Anyone with Internet access could just Google either her name or Drake's Designs and get the information that they needed instantaneously. Breathing a sigh of relief Mileena set the letter aside, and briefly mulled over the idea of actually giving it to her sister, then went through the rest of the day's mail.

"If I may say." The event planner began in a stuffy tone. "This little yard of yours may be just **too** small to properly celebrate a wedding reception in, in my estimation." She emphasized waving her well manicured and bejeweled hands around as she surveyed Holly and Mark's backyard with obvious contempt.

And of course, it had just rained an hour prior to this meeting; leaving everything wet and unaccommodating to someone who chose to wear 4 inch stiletto heals! Holly took an instant dislike to this woman the moment that she laid eyes on her, and reluctantly let her into her home. At first blush, Erica Pennington of "Pennington's Precious Day Planners" was completely over the top. For starters she was dressed as if it were eighty-five degrees outside; wearing a white floral sleeveless sundress with matching sun hat and briefcase. The large hat also sported a huge yellow chrysanthemum on the right side. Holly assumed that Erica wanted to convey a "wedding feel" to her appearance. But to Holly she just appeared to be ridiculous. And from what she could tell completely out of her element. "Take this filthy bird bath for instance." She began as she wobbled in the wet grass nearing one of Holly's most treasured backyard items. "Ugh! This simply has got to go!" Erica exclaimed as if she had just tasted something disgusting. "I like that birdbath." Holly began through gritted teeth. "It was a gift from my sister." She stated as she folded her arms close to her chest. "Mmm, yes."

Erica commented looking away from the "dreadful" birdbath. Holly watched as the woman stumbled, tripped, and nearly made a spectacle of herself as she canvassed the entire yard valiantly searching for a way to make Holly and Mark's pathetic little space into a wedding reception splendor. "Well!" Erica began out of breath from her whirlwind trip around the slippery area. "I must admit this will be quite a challenge should I decide to make a contract with you for your little reception." She exclaimed while hurriedly rummaging around in her purse for, what Holly could only image to be, something to wipe off the middle class filth of the day. Holly would have to call Mileena later and thank her for the wonderful event planner recommendation!

Requisite Shadows

Mark sat in his truck curiously watching a new home being constructed over the empty site that was once occupied by the home of Trevor Morgan. His mind quickly reeled back to that fateful day when he and Mileena had searched valiantly for Holly, ending up right at this very spot and not knowing whether Holly was alive or dead. Mark shuddered to think of what would have happened were he and Mileena just a few minutes later in arriving. He would be lost without his beautiful Holly. Mark had waited so long to finally be with her, and he knew in his heart of hearts that his life would be absolutely nothing without her. Mark just wished that he would have had the opportunity to meet Trevor face to face and after the fact. "In just one second buddy you would have known what pain truly was." Mark breathed. But Mark never had the chance to confront Trevor. Trevor's life ended abruptly that ominous afternoon. Mark was about to put his truck into gear and head home when something caught his eye. A man was standing silently not far from the construction site, and just behind a small pile of building materials. The strange man didn't seem to be associated with the construction crew as he wore a long black trench coat and what seemed to be a simple suit beneath. He also held an unopened black umbrella in his hand. Mark thought that was strange as it was now starting to rain a little harder than it had this morning. Mark craned his neck looking through his wet windshield and tried to make out who he may be, but then concluded that he was either an overseer of the construction process or quite possibly the new home owner checking out the construction's progress.

"Jeez now I'm becoming paranoid!" Mark thought anxiously as he began driving slowly past the home and then making quick eye contact with the stranger. A short chill ran down Mark's spine as the stranger locked stares with him. He was unflinching and intense. Mark nodded to the man as he passed, but was not given the courtesy of a return nod. The man's concentrated stare followed Mark as he passed. Just then his cell phone rang. Mark gingerly pulled his truck onto the shoulder of the road and looked at his cell. It was Holly. "Hello my beautiful bride to be. How did things go this morning?" Mark answered breathing a sigh of relief as he listened to Holly. "Well, I have to tell you. That party planner that Mileena recommended was something to see." She giggled. Mark loved Holly's giggle. It was contagious. "I may look into other party planners if it's all the same with you honey." Holly conveyed knowing that she was never going to book their special day with that awful woman. "Well if you have to Holly but we only have a few weeks left to wrap this stuff up." Mark warned as he looked up into his rearview mirror. Startled, he noticed the man from the construction site had moved into the street to watch Mark's departure. He was just standing in the center of the road and facing in Mark's direction. "Ah Holly, my phone's starting to cut out sweetie. Can we talk when I get home?" Mark asked starting to pull away from the shoulder and onto the road. The stranger remained in the middle of the road unwavering. Mark started to drive home and watched for as long as he could safely; the dark stranger in his rearview mirror.

As Holly set the table for dinner her phone rang. "Hello?" She sang out happily knowing that Mark was due home any minute. "Hey Holly it's Mil." Mileena began. "How's the wedding plans coming along?" Holly burst out laughing. "I was just about to call you Mil and tell you just how it's going!' She began. "I have to ask you sis, where in the world did you find Pennington's Precious Day Planners!" She laughed hard again. "Why? What happened?" Mileena asked knowing that some of her stylists used Erica Pennington for many of their special occasions. "Well, for one thing she showed up here dressed like she's going to a tea party in August and then she was so damn condescending that I could have strangled her." Holly ranted. "She's definitely NOT going to be taking care of my wedding reception I can tell you that much." Holly remarked. "I'm so sorry Holly. Really I am. She came so highly recommended. You know that I want only the best for ya Sis." Mileena assured her. "I know Mil. Don't sweat it. I still have a few weeks left. I'm sure there are other good people out there that will get the job done without making me feel like a second class citizen." Holly giggled. As the girls got caught up on everything Mileena's cell phone rang. She glanced quickly at it and noticed an unfamiliar number so she let it go to her voicemail for later. "You wanna come over for dinner tonight Mil? I'm making enchiladas, one of your favorites." Holly asked missing her sister who she hadn't seen in a few weeks. Mileena knew in her heart that if she were to see her sister now, Holly would pick up on how Mileena was feeling about the letter, and question her endlessly about it.

She just wasn't prepared mentally yet to tell Holly about it. Mileena wanted to wait until after the wedding and when everything had quieted down before she would let Holly and Mark know what was going on. "Not tonight Holly. I've got a late night at the shop and then Rocky is picking me up for a late dinner." Holly was struck. This was the third offer that Mileena had turned down in as many weeks. "Okay Mil. No problem. But I should be going now as Mark will be home any minute now." Mileena hated disappointing her sister but she just wasn't ready. And since Mileena knew that the sender of the letter was in no way able to find Holly, there'd be no trouble just yet. "Okay Holly. Talk to you later." Mileena finished hanging up. Remembering that she had received a call while she and Holly were on the phone, Mileena grabbed her cell phone and listened to her missed message. "Good evening Mileena. This is Ian Morgan. I am calling to find out whether or not you have given your sister my letter yet." Mileena physically blanched and sat back hard against the couch. "Judging by the lapse of time that has transpired, and no response from Holly,

I'm assuming that the answer to that would be no." Mileena's heart began thumping wildly in her chest as she listened to the remainder of the message. "I highly suggest that you give Holly my letter, and instruct her to call me immediately Mileena. No one gets away with murdering my brother."

Ian Morgan ate his meal slowly and watched the Sunday lunch crowd begin to filter into the small but pleasant downtown restaurant; that was modeled loosely after the television show "Cheers". Ian liked this place best out of all the other restaurants he had frequented. He was able to sit at the windows that faced the picturesque street, lined with quaint shops and eateries, and he could watch all the town's activity comfortably. Upon learning of his brother's ghastly murder Ian flew immediately to Michigan from New York City. Ian never acknowledged Trevor's son Christopher. "The bastard son of a whore." As he so often referred to the little boy. Ian wasn't much into children viewing them as financial burdens. After locating this tiny town of Milford, Ian sequestered himself at a nice hotel just a mile or two from town. And in Ian's room was the front page story from the local paper of the whole event of last January's fire. In Ian's mind the local reporters put such a spin on that story that it absolutely infuriated him. To think that Trevor was in any way responsible for that fire or the torture and rape of his ex-wife Holly Andrews, was absolutely ludicrous. Anyone who knew Holly Andrews knew that she was unstable. A highly emotional woman who in Ian's opinion was drawn to drama in every aspect of her life. Ian met Holly while attending her and Trevor's wedding. And his opinion of Holly from the beginning was not favorable. Trevor could have and should have done far better in his selection of a wife. And now that Holly was responsible, in Ian's mind, for the loss of his brother he was going to see to it that she be made to pay. He wouldn't kill her though. Ian had too much at stake back home in New York. And to jeopardize all that he had amassed with a murder sentence just would not make sense to him. "Would you like today's paper to read with your lunch sir?" A lovely waitress inquired softly. "That would be nice. Thank you my dear." Ian answered taking the paper.

"Well, how are you feeling Mrs. Harris?" Mark emphasized with pleasure as he and Holly rode home together from their recent nuptials at City Hall to their home in a rented limousine. "I could not be happier Mark! I love being your wife!" Holly exclaimed leaning towards Mark and kissing him fully on the lips. "You are absolutely stunning my love." Mark replied as he looked at his new wife as if for the very first time. "Here we are!" Mark exclaimed as the limo pulled in front of their house. Holly noticed right away that the front door was ornately decorated with white and yellow ribbons, little white doves, and a dozen or more wedding-themed balloons. A large white banner was draped over the entrance and in large script letters read, "Congratulations Holly and Mark!" As Mark took Holly's hand and pulled her slowly from the limo, her heart swelled with love and pride as she took Mark's hand and stood next to him momentarily. The photographer was immediately by their side snapping photos and exclaiming his approval of the lovely bride and her handsome husband. When the photographer had his fill, the newly married couple strode confidently up the front walk and into their home.

Ian couldn't believe his luck! Right there upon the pages of the newspaper he was just recently handed, was the information that he truly needed to begin his dance with Holly Andrews; now Mrs. Holly Harris. Ian eyed the rather large wedding announcement picture of Holly and her new husband Mark.

Holly truly was a beautiful woman, but Ian knew to tread lightly with her.

By now, and with all that recently transpired, Holly would be a very suspicious woman along with all her other emotional issues. Ian needed to return to his room and continue with his plans. Plans that would teach Holly a very valuable lesson.

It was late into the evening and the guests had long departed including Mileena and Rocky. Holly and Mark were still sitting silently in their private Gazebo enjoying the evening's cool breezes and tranquil splendor. The grandfather clock, not far away in the living room, began gently chiming and would not finish until it reached twelve chimes. Baby white lights, hidden deeply in the surrounding trees, twinkled delicately and reminded Holly of a night long passed when she had gone camping with friends and the sky was completely laden with stars. Mark watched Holly as she appeared deeply enchanted with all that had transpired this day. She was absolutely glowing with love and tranquility. He knew that this night was the beginning of their story together. A never-ending romance where the lead male would die a most happy man in the end. "It's getting late my love, aren't you tired?" Mark asked in a purposeful manner. Holly slowly brought her attention from the fairyland around her to her gorgeous new husband. He looked magnificent. Still dressed in his sharp black tuxedo, but with the bow tie slightly askew. His five o'clock shadow was becoming obvious but Holly thought that only added to his virility. "Yes Mark, let's go inside now." She whispered smiling, then stood slowly taking one last look around her. "Mileena did such a wonderful job for us tonight Mark." Holly commented as they strolled together towards the house.

"She really came through when I needed her." She conveyed as she felt Mark's strong hand slowly stroke her back. "Mileena will always be there for you Holly." Mark began as they walked through the kitchen. "She is a good sister and a true friend." Holly stopped momentarily and stood facing Mark. "Why don't you go turn down the bed my love and I will go slip into something more appropriate." She breathed. Mark watched as Holly slowly moved away from him, glancing back seductively, and then sauntered towards their bedroom and into the adjoining bathroom. His heart swelled with pride and his hunger for Holly grew quickly. Ripping his tuxedo coat off and throwing it to the floor, Mark quickly followed his wife's gentle footsteps down the hall.

It was late into the evening and Ian was still awake and working at the desk in his hotel room. From all that he had gathered from his friends back home, Holly's background was relatively clean; with the exception of a few speeding tickets here and there. Ian was rather surprised to learn that Holly held a Bachelor's degree in Biology and had taught for a very brief stint at Mariner High School. He never figured Holly as having that much intelligence packed away in such an emotionally occupied brain. Smiling, Ian grabbed a local telephone directory out of the hotel's desk drawer and began thumbing swiftly through the yellow pages. Finding the information he sought, he wrote briefly on a piece of paper and returned the directory to the desk drawer. In the morning he would have some errands to run and a few people to talk to.

Mileena was exhausted, and upon rising the next morning she was actually glad that all of the excitement from Holly and Mark's wedding reception last night was over.

Holly never looked more beautiful or more happy in Mileena's estimation. Mark would be good for her sister and Holly would need him now more than ever. Mileena's thoughts then drew back to the phone call that she received from Ian. She knew this man was to be taken very seriously. In the letter he only asked that he be granted the opportunity to talk to Holly. Mileena could gather that the conversation he intended to have with Holly had absolutely nothing to do with pleasantries and everything to do with his dead brother Trevor. She had to decide on a time very soon to reveal this information to Holly. She had tried several times already, making futile attempts to take the letter to Holly and Mark's house, but chickened out before talking to either of them. If Ian was even remotely as crazy as his brother Trevor, they were all in for some real trouble.

"Welcome to Mariner High Mr. Morgan". The assistant principle called out from his behind his desk and upon seeing Ian walk into the reception office of the High School. He immediately stood and made his way out of his office and towards the bank of clerical desks that faced the front of the school's administration office. "I'm Jonas Seering the Assistant Principle." Ian walked purposefully towards the short, balding man and shook his hand affably. Ian had arrived promptly at their scheduled meeting time dressed appropriately in a dark blue three piece suit and tie. In his right hand he carried a fashionable brief case and in his left the morning newspaper. "You're a busy man Mr. Seering. I don't suppose you've had a chance to read this morning's paper." Ian began handing the assistant principle a fresh copy. "Well, that's mighty kind of you Mr. Morgan. Mighty kind." "Please won't you join me in my office."

The two men made their way back through the reception office and into Jonas's office. "Have a seat Mr. Morgan and we can begin." Jonas began as he lumbered slowly around his desk. Upon finding his own seat, he sat gingerly with a soft grunt. "Please, call me Ian." Ian began as he surveyed the tidy little office and becoming pleased that his plans now had motion to them.

The phone was ringing on the nightstand beside Holly and Mark's bed. Mark rolled over slowly with his eyes still closed and tried to decide if he wanted to answer it. Holly moaned softly next to him and switched her position. She looked so peaceful and lovely as she slept. Mark grabbed the phone then and hoarsely answered it. "Mmm hello?" He asked sleepily.

"Hi Mark. It's Mileena". She began shakily. "Is Holly up yet?" Mark slowly and cautiously got out of bed and walked out of the bedroom then quickly down the hall. "No Mil." He whispered softly. "She's sleeping. We were up very late last night celebrating." Mark answered rubbing his eyes and continuing down the hall into the kitchen. "What's up?" He asked as he reached the kitchen and then started to prepare a pot of coffee. Mileena sat almost suspended in time. Should she tell Mark now about Ian's letter? Had she waited long enough? "Oh it's nothing major hun. I was just wondering how Holly's night went. You know, girl talk." She answered slightly unsure of her voice. "I'll have her call you when she gets up Mil. Shouldn't be too much longer." Mark assured. Glancing at the kitchen clock he noticed that it was ten o'clock and probably a good time to start some breakfast for new his bride. "Okay, thank you Mark." Mileena replied. "Goodbye hun."

Mileena sat holding the receiver and cursing to herself. She should have told Mark everything while Holly slept. That way Mark could have explained everything to Holly himself. Though Holly would have been shocked and upset at first, at least she would have her big strong husband there for assurance. Together they could have worked things out, and Mileena would not have this burden to worry about anymore. Mileena just hoped and prayed that she would have the strength for yet another round in Holly's life battles.

Deception's Red Herring

Paul Murphy stirred groggily and shifted his large frame in the unyielding airplane seat. The 747 had just landed and was rolling smoothly and effortlessly down the runway. Shaking his head slightly and glancing out the tiny oval window, Paul yawned broadly. It was a brief flight from New York's La Guardia airport to Detroit's Metropolitan Airport, but Paul had been up most of the night before on the telephone discussing business matters with his boss.

Paul watched as the outlying buildings, idle and transferring planes, and airport markers flew by his tiny window; then gradually slowed along with the plane's pace. He glanced openly at his watch noticing that the flight was right on schedule. Below his feet he had stashed his brief case containing the many essentials that he would be needing for this brief trip. Rummaging into his pants pocket he retrieved his cell phone and turned it on. After a brief moment the phone's neon face lit up and the phone beeped with power recognition. Another similar beep sounded indicating that he had an unheard voicemail. Paul ignored it and shoved the phone back into his pants. He intended to get off this plane, find his luggage, and secure a vehicle for the long drive that lay ahead of him; hopefully all without a lot of fan fair. "Good morning ladies and gentleman." A man's jovial voice began. "This is your pilot Captain Jimmy Marsh. I'd like to welcome you to Detroit's Metropolitan Airport. The weather here in the Motor City this morning is cloudy with a seventy percent chance of rain. Hope you all brought your umbrellas!" Paul glanced forward and rolled his eyes. "Quite the comedian for nine o'clock in the morning." He thought annoyed.

Many passengers were already on their feet and hauling out their belongings from beneath their seats or out of the overhead compartments. Paul waited in his seat impatiently. He hated this part of traveling by air the most. When everyone was in such a rush to get off the plane. Paul knew that no matter how hard you tried or prepared for there was always someone who was slow, or was juggling a few too many bags, or struggling with a few kicking and screaming kids. It would become a cattle call in the next few minutes and he would have nothing to do with it. Paul did not deal well with stress nor impatience. And as he watched the seemingly endless stream of humanity pass by him his cell phone rang. Reaching in and grabbing the phone he impatiently answered it. "Paul Murphy." He growled running his hand through his hair. "I see you've made it to Detroit." Ian began. "After you've retrieved your luggage a car will be waiting for you outside of the departures building. There will also be a map in the glove compartment indicating your route to my hotel. I will see you here in an hour." Paul flipped the phone closed and rose to his feet. The line was thinning and he was able to slowly squeeze out of his seat and into the narrow aisle. As he followed along with the crowd's snail like pace, Paul remembered the fax that he received from Ian last night. He would meet with Ian at his hotel first and then afterwards a lunch meeting with Jonas Seering. The tips of Paul's full mouth moved into a slight smile as he never quite thought of himself as the principle of a Midwestern High School.

Paul Murphy was an dangerously handsome man. Born from Irish parents he took on all the remarkable aspects of the nationality. Wavy dark blonde hair, bright blue eyes that were full of soul and laden with that unmistakable glint of devilment, and a generous smile that could light up a room. Paul was a formidable man at well over six feet tall and with a frame that was muscular and capable. When he talked he did so with a quick wit and spoke with an undeniable city accent that was coupled with a slight brogue reflective of his lineage. Paul had managed over the years to melt and break many a heart on the east coast. Which was reason number one why Ian had chosen him for this "special project.".

"Who was that on the phone baby?" Holly asked Mark as she emerged from the hallway and into the kitchen. Still in last night's baby doll pajamas she meandered slowly over to her new husband and kissed him fully and deeply on his lips. Mark responded immediately by wrapping his strong arms around her and pulling her delicate frame against him. She smelled luscious. A scent so familiar to him that it drove him wild to be near her. "You smell good enough to eat Holly." Mark groaned. His breath was hot against her neck and sent chills down Holly's back and legs. She moaned and clung to Mark as he began kissing and nibbling her neck and bare shoulder. Holly's hands took hold of Mark's head and she brought his face to hers so that she could share his taste. Their kissing became hotter and stronger as Holly felt Mark promptly lift her into his arms. He carried her for a short way before laying her gently upon the living room couch.

"You are mine Holly." Mark breathed with fevered intent. "Forever mine." He finished as he quickly stripped out of his boxer shorts and joined his wife. He carefully pulled down her panties as she pulled off her filmy top. They lay naked together exploring one another as if for the first time. "Never leave me Mark." Holly groaned as Mark's hands worked their magic upon her breasts.

"Never!" Mark promised through gritted teeth as he gently kissed her exposed breasts and made his way down Holly's warm and silky belly. Holly was on fire as never before. Every inch of her body was tingling and blooming. Her mind reeling from every delicious sensation. She was now finally free of the past. Free of Trevor and all that had occurred between them. Her beloved Mark had healed her from everything that had torn her apart. Mark entered Holly then with reckless abandon; driving into her fluidly and with fierce and wild passion. Holly gripped the couch cushions tightly as she wrapped her quivering legs firmly around his waist; her entire body embracing her treasured soul mate. Suddenly Mark turned and brought Holly upon him. Holly cried out in rapture as she was swathed in the deepest passion that she had ever experienced. Sparks danced about in her ardent visions as Holly surrendered herself to Mark. The two becoming one body, one soul.

Paul pulled his rental car into the parking lot of the Huron Motor Inn and cut the engine. As Ian indicated, it was a dreadfully long drive from the airport and Paul being more accustomed to city life was not prepared for the extended journey. He was tired, hungry, and a little more than aggravated. Taking a quick glance at the map Paul noticed Ian's room number scribbled at the top of the page. Retrieving his briefcase from the rider's side seat he exited the car and strode promptly up to Ian's room. The door stood ajar as Paul neared the room. He thought that strange and instinctively hesitated for a moment just outside the door. "Come in, come in!" Ian bellowed from somewhere inside the room.

Paul stepped through the doorway to find Ian sitting at a small desk, smoking a cigarette, and going over paperwork. "Do you always leave the door standing wide open Ian?" Paul asked setting his briefcase on the nearest bed and glancing around the small but quaint room. "The fresh air is invigorating Paul and besides we are in the Midwest. No one locks their doors or closes their windows around here." Ian remarked getting to his feet and greeting his friend. The two shook hands vigorously and exchanged a brief hug. Ian and Paul were of the same age and came from similar backgrounds.

They both graduated from Lafayette High School in Brooklyn, New York and were raised in the surrounding area of Bensonhurst. Several years after graduating their neighborhood came under siege when it made national headlines. A young 16-year-old boy was attacked by an angry mob of youths from that neighborhood. One of whom, armed with a handgun, shot and killed the young boy. It was hard times for Ian and Paul, but after a long stint with the law, unemployment, and hardship, the two put their heads together and came up with a plan for their futures that was both lucrative and stable. "So Principle Murphy how was the drive in?" Ian asked with an obvious mocking tone. Paul had to laugh despite his annoyed state. "Long!" He barked. "Long and lonely." All the vast farming landscapes and little towns that Paul had passed on his way in made him yearn for, if nothing else, conversation. Paul was a Leo born man and loved to be surrounded by friends and acquaintances. He also yearned for the love of a good woman. But good women were few and far between in Paul's estimation. He resigned himself to the fact long ago that you couldn't trust anyone in this world to make you happy. "Well, you've got a meeting with Jonas Seering in about an hour to go over the niceties and then I'll meet you later for dinner so we can tie up any loose ends." Ian instructed. Ian figured that just about now Holly would be getting a life changing phone call. Ian also knew that Mileena would no longer be suspicious of him and would live the rest of her days as if this whole matter no longer was a threat to her precious sister.

Mileena sat at her office desk and reread the recent letter that Ian had just recently sent to her home. It struck her rather odd that he did not call her like he did the last time and explain his hasty departure and subsequent return home, but either way she was satisfied that Ian had a change of heart and was now leaving Michigan all-together. Mileena rose from her desk and tossed the letter into the garbage bucket near the desk. She then began the descent down to the main floor of her salon knowing in her heart that Holly and Mark could now be finally free of the past, of the devastation that Trevor Morgan had caused, and that neither of them would know of the beginnings of something that never quite came to fruition. She smiled then while watching her very busy salon filled with happy and satisfied customers. Drake's Design's was absolutely booming with energy. Of course her selection of music only helped add to the excited environment. Every morning before she opened her shop Mileena selected her salon's music for the day. Today's vibe was "Dirty" by Christina Aguilera and boomed through out the building. Mileena also noticed, with a quickening heart, her love Rocky walking through the front door as he glanced around looking for her. Upon seeing Mileena, Rocky walked steadily and confidently over to her. "Looks like you've got a full day ahead of you Mileena." He began as he bent down and planted a warm kiss on her exposed neck. His warm full lips sent chills all over Mileena's body. "Indeed it does." She began. "But I wonder hun. Do you have plans for lunch today?" She asked purposefully. Knowing her implications, Rocky took Mileena's hand in his. "Depends on what's being served." He replied with a wicked grin.

As Holly and Mark ate breakfast together, eyeing each other playfully, the phone in the kitchen rang. "I got it!" Mark stated getting up from his chair and headed into the kitchen. He was still naked from earlier that morning and Holly watched his muscular back, buttocks, and legs move away from her. "God he's gorgeous!" She thought as she sipped her coffee. She was now Holly Harris. Married one full day. Coming back from her delicious thoughts she saw Mark heading towards her with the phone in his hand. "It's for you baby. It's Mariner High School." Holly's jaw dropped as she shakily set her coffee cup down and sat gaping at her husband. Her mind was working a thousand miles an hour. What could they possibly want with her? Holly figured that she would never hear from them again after all that had happened last year. She figured fired was fired and that would be the end of it. Did she leave something behind with her hasty departure? Holly looked at Mark and mouthed the words, "What do they want?" Mark grinned from ear to ear as he covered the phone with his hand. "I don't know Holly" He whispered. "But I think the only way to find out would be for you to take the call." He laughed handing Holly the phone. "Hello? This is Holly Andrews...um I mean Holly Harris." She laughed not quite used to her new last name yet. "Good morning Holly. This is Jonas Seering the assistant principle of Mariner High School. How are you this morning?" He asked in a cheery tone. "I'm fine Mr. Seering, but a little surprised to hear from you." Holly began in a tone that was a little shakier than she would have liked. "What can I do for you?" Holly asked grabbing Mark's hand, who had taken a seat next to her for support. "Well I'd like to make a proposal to you and offer you your old job back. That is if you are still available?" Holly was floored! She couldn't believe her luck. One of the worst things that had ever happened to her in her life was losing her Biology teaching position at Mariner High. And now she had the opportunity to seize hold of it again and show her colleagues what a great teacher she really was. She stared at Mark with a shocked and happy expression on her lovely face. "My old job back really?" She asked merely to see Mark's response. Mark smiled broadly and kissed the top of Holly's hand. "Indeed." Jonas responded. "We also have a new principle here. His name is Paul Murphy and just the nicest man." Holly couldn't believe it. Things were turning around for her. "I'd be delighted to come by Jonas and discuss this with you further today If you have time for me that is?" She asked hating to do business over the phone. "That would be perfect Holly. How about two o'clock? By that time Mr. Murphy will have returned from lunch and we can all get acquainted." He replied. Holly, trying hard not to have a giggle fit, squeezed Mark's hand lovingly. "That would be fine Jonas. I will see you today at two o'clock." She answered.

Holly laid the phone down on the kitchen table and grabbed a hold of Mark. "I can't believe it!" She squealed. "I'm getting my teaching job back!" She cried.

Mark and Holly held each other close feeling that now that the world was their oyster, and that nothing nor no one would ever muddle their world again.

"It's done." Jonas replied hanging up the phone. "We will all meet here in my office at two o'clock." He replied. "Fine". Paul started. "I'm off to grab some lunch now and will see you back here later." He finished grabbing his briefcase and heading out of Jonas's office. Once out of the building and into the school's front courtyard and safely out of earshot, Paul placed a call to Ian. "It's started Ian." He relayed then closed his cell phone with a snap and returned it to his pants pocket. Paul noticed several women teachers were standing just off to his side and were watching him intently. One lovely blonde slowly raised her hand and gave a slight wave. Paul nodded and then made steady eye contact with the young beauty. She was striking for a teacher. Tall, slim and slightly tanned. Her blonde hair was curled slightly and shined in the afternoon sun. He would have to make his acquaintance with her soon. Paul knew that all of the women that were gathered here, were gossiping about his appearance at the school today and wondering if he were the new principle. "Good afternoon ladies!" Paul called out for good measure. "Beautiful day." He replied and kept walking towards the parking lot. He heard a few responses, but mostly hushed giggles. "This little project of Ian's could actually become rather enjoyable." Paul thought to himself as he opened the car door and tossed in his briefcase.

"I can't believe it!" Holly squealed with delight. "Oh Mark I'm going to be teaching again!" She shrieked.

Holly was beside herself with happiness. Everything was going to be fine now. Mark glanced at his watch while Holly cleared the breakfast table. "What time are you supposed to be at the school?" He asked seeing it was twelve o'clock. "Two o'clock. So as soon as I'm finished here I'm going to go jump in the shower and then figure out what I'm going to wear to knock their socks off!" She giggled while carrying an armload of dishes into the kitchen. "You want some help with that Holly?" Mark asked nearing the table. "No, hun I think I've cleared the table." Holly answered as she began humming to herself. Mark was suddenly behind her and circling his strong arms around her waist.. "I didn't mean the dishes Holly. I meant the shower." He breathed into her neck.

Ian, now pleased with how his little process was going, decided to venture out and look for more suitable accommodations for himself and Paul. His hotel room, though nice and quiet, was inappropriate for two grown men and also for an extended period of time. While Paul was at his meeting with the assistant principle at Mariner High Ian spoke with a realtor who specialized in short term housing rentals in town. And to his surprise the realtor indicated that one property was available for immediate occupancy; should Ian agree to the terms. Ian drove only for a short period of time before finding the neighborhood that the realtor had directed him to. Upon finding the designated dwelling, a two bedroom bungalow style home, Ian spied the realtor standing beside a car that was parked in the home's driveway. The neighborhood was quiet beautiful; Ian grudgingly had to admit to himself. And so much different from the city streets and sounds that he loved and was used to. These picturesque suburban streets were lined with many maple trees, laden with deep green leaves. Deep green evergreen trees stood like sentries in some of the yards and must have grown to heights of well over 15 feet. Ian knew that they would most likely be decorated this holiday season with blinking lights and perhaps a few ornaments.

The home owners of this community took great pride in their landscaping and also the upkeep of their homes. "Mr. Morgan!" The realtor called out upon seeing Ian park and then exit his car along the street. Ian approached the man and briskly shook his rather wimpy grip. "I'm Bob Brown from Lakes Realty." The realtor looked to Ian to be about 45, lanky build, and slightly balding. He wore dress pants and a polo shirt in the same color of beige and carried with him a thick white file folder under his arm. Ian, as always, was impeccably dressed in a designer suit and tie. "Nice to make your acquaintance Mr. Brown." Ian began. "Beautiful neighborhood." He finished and waited for the realtor to begin the process. "Oh yes it is! One of the nicest in Waterford Township." He stated with obvious pride. "Shall we go inside Mr. Morgan?" He asked with a gesture for Ian to follow him. "I think you will find this home to your liking Mr. Morgan." The realtor conveyed. Ian followed the man silently as his eyes moved around the perimeter of the home. "How long will you be staying with us sir?" The realtor pried as he unlocked the front door and motioned for Ian to enter. Ian stepped through the entryway and into the foyer of the home. The home was completely empty and void of any existence of a previous owner. Highly polished hardwood floors throughout, reflected the beautiful sunshine that shone through every window. Ian was impressed. Whoever lived here before took very good care of this home. "I have an open-ended ticket in my pocket Mr. Brown." Ian began slightly forced at being picked and prodded at for information. "I will remain in Michigan until I have finished my business here." The realtor seemed oblivious to Ian's implications. "I can't detect your accent Mr. Morgan. Where are you from by chance?" He asked as the two walked into the spacious living room.

Ian ignored the realtor and walked passed him and into the living room; coming to a stop at two large French doors that looked out onto a small deck. The backyard, that was dotted with heavy maple trees, came after the deck and protectively wrapped the yard on three sides with a fence. "I'll take it." Ian stated. "My partner and I will move in this weekend."

Holly pulled her car into the parking lot of Mariner High School and kept the engine running and the music on inside. She sat for a bit and forced her nerves to quiet. It had been almost a year since she had taught here and Holly still could not believe that she was given another chance to do so. Exiting her car she fought back the horrific memories that were still nudging at her brain. "It's different now." She began aloud. "Trevor is gone and buried and so with him the memories be." She finished repeating a mantra that Mark had given her when she was faced with a difficult situation. Once inside the school Holly located the administration office and went inside. Everything was exactly as it was before. "May I help you?" A young lady inquired of Holly. "I have an appointment to see Mr. Seering at two o'clock. I'm Holly Harris." God she loved saying her new name to anyone who would listen! "Just one moment please."

The woman cautioned then rose fluidly and walked back to the assistant principle's office. Holly's stomach was filled with very animated butterflies that simply refused to behave; regardless of Mark's endless mantras. Even though Holly knew Jonas Seering this was still a difficult hurdle to get over, she hoped that he would not pry too heavily into the "who's and what's" of her past and just get on with the business at hand. "Holly!" Jonas called out from his office.

"Come on back!" He shouted while gesturing for Holly to proceed through the office. Holly walked somewhat steadily passed the administrative secretaries and into Jonas's office. The women of the office all eyed her curiously, as if trying to remember just where they had seen this woman before. "We are almost ready to begin Holly. Please have a seat." Jonas instructed as Holly entered the office. "We are waiting for Paul Murphy who should be here any minute." Holly sat in the nearest seat and wondered about this new principle. She got along rather well with the previous principle and was interested to know why he was no longer employed at the school. "Would you like some coffee Holly, or perhaps water?" Jonas asked as he sat behind his desk. "No thank you Jonas. I'm fine." Holly replied nervously. She could just imagine trying to juggle something to drink with hands that she knew would most likely betray her. "Ah here he comes now!"

Jonas replied seeing Paul approaching his office. Holly turned around in her seat and watched him near the room. She started quivering mildly in her seat. Holly was completely taken off guard and as she stood to greet Paul Murphy, she found herself wobbly on her feet. He was stunning! And far too good looking to be a principle she felt. He was tall, handsome and boldly confident in his demeanor. "Good afternoon." Paul began as he entered the office. Then turning to Holly, "You must be Holly Harris." He began extending his hand to Holly. "I'm Paul Murphy. The new principle here at Mariner High." His voice was warm and with a slight east coast accent that Holly couldn't quite put her finger on just yet. Holly took his hand in hers and couldn't help but stare with amazement at Paul's eyes. They were blue, but not just run-of-the-mill blue. They had flecks of green and gold.

Black eyelashes rimmed these ocular beauties. His hair was short, but slightly wavy, and dark blonde. And when he smiled at her she felt something stir within. He was captivating. And exactly the reason why Ian had chosen him for this matter. "Hello Paul it's nice to meet you." Holly answered quickly letting go of his hand. Paul continued to stare at Holly with a look that could not have been mistaken. "Shall we begin?" Jonas asked unaware as he situated himself comfortably and grabbed a large folder. Holly sat gingerly back into the chair that she chose at her arrival, as Paul pulled up a chair close to her and sat down as well. Holly now wished she would have asked Mark to accompany her. She needed his strong energy right now. As Jonas began explaining to Holly his proposal for her future employment at the school, she could just feel Paul's intense stare upon her. "This isn't the way I imagined this meeting to go." Holly thought worriedly. "They didn't make Principles like this when I was a kid." She mused. "As you know Holly I arranged for us to have this meeting to discuss your further employment here at Mariner High." Jonas began in a stately way. Holly's attention was now fully on Jonas. "Yes, and I am very interested to hear what you have to say." Holly stated as she tried not to think about Paul's obvious interest. "Well as I see it Holly, you had just started your employment here when…" Jonas began as he fumbled quickly through the file. "When you suddenly quit without warning and no explanation given to anyone." Holly had a feeling that she would have to explain herself. Trial by fire. But she also wished that it were just she and Jonas who were discussing this point in her life.

"That's right Jonas. My husband Mark, who was my boyfriend at the time, was brutally attacked by my ex-husband Trevor Morgan." Holly began, fighting against the anxiety that was quickly welling up within her. "Mark had no immediate family members to take care of him once he was released from the hospital, and I felt obligated to nurse him back to health." Holly finished visibly shaking from head to toe. Jonas sat quietly listening to her when his expression changed. "Wait a minute." He began. "I remember now. I read about that whole incident in the paper. They even ran a few segments about that on the local news channel." He relayed. Holly's body was as stiff as a board. Did they have to revisit the whole incident right here and right now? "Yes, now it's clear." Jonas continued, "And your ex-husband actually died in the house fire shortly there after." Holly's mind reeled and she began shaking from head to toe. Paul quickly noticed Holly's composure failing and interceded. "Jonas, I believe we all know the story." Even though Paul quite didn't. Ian was very vague when it came to all the details as to why he was out for revenge with Holly. "And it's obvious to me that this is still a very touchy subject with Holly. I suggest that we let go of this terrible story and get on with the hiring process." He commanded flatly feeling almost sorry for Holly and her obvious past torment. Holly looked at Paul and whispered, "Thank you Paul." Paul nodded and they continued with the meeting. "Very well." Jonas began. "When are you available to start Holly?"

All the way home Holly tried desperately to clear her head of the horrifying period she spent with Trevor Morgan and back to the reality of the reinstatement of her job. What Holly struggled with now was Paul Murphy.

Maybe she was just nervous and was taking him the wrong way but the vibe she felt from him was unmistakable. And completely inappropriate on Paul's part. Holly wondered if he was married. Paul and Jonas both knew that Holly was newly married so there should be no question in Paul's mind that she was off the market. And what principle behaves so boldly? Holly wondered if Jonas had picked up on Paul's obvious interest. Holly desperately needed to get home now and relax. To be with her beloved husband Mark. He would make things all better. He always did.

Paul pulled along side the small diner that sat adjacent to the main street in town. He immediately saw Ian's car parked several cars ahead of his. Paul was exhausted. It had been a long day since landing at the airport this morning. It was now four o'clock and he was ready for a stiff drink and an early dinner.

Ian had filled Paul in briefly while he was still in New York; about what he expected Paul to accomplish with Holly. And Paul was slightly puzzled as to why Ian was going to such great lengths to destroy a woman he barely knew. The only reason was revenge. Ian's revenge against a woman he assumed was responsible for his brother's death. But unbeknownst to Ian, Paul had done some research on his own into Ian's brother's life as well as Holly's life; when Ian first posed his plan to him. Paul had discovered among many things that Trevor Morgan had a long history of domestic violence, had a lengthy arrest record, and had indeed kidnapped and brutally raped Holly last year. But who was Paul to question Ian's actions? He never did and he never would. Ian's plans were always very lucrative for Paul.

And Paul would never be hungry nor broke ever again. His life was very comfortable thanks to Ian and all Paul had to do was to take care of business for Ian. Ian was the brains and Paul was the brawn. Paul found Ian sitting at a small table by the front windows. He was reading the local paper and sipping a drink. Paul grabbed the seat across from Ian and abruptly sat down with a long sigh. "Well, my friend." Ian began with a slightly thicker brogue. "The dance has begun now, hasn't it now?"

"There's she is!" Mark exclaimed upon seeing Holly skip through the front door. She was a picture of happiness and Mark couldn't take his eyes off of her. "Oh Mark!" Holly gushed. "I start Monday!" She exclaimed running to Mark and embracing him tightly. Mark quickly wrapped his arms around Holly and held her closely against him. Her hair smelled like a mix of her perfume and the outdoor air. Mark stuck his nose in her hair and breathed in her familiar scent; which calmed him instantly. All afternoon Mark wondered about how Holly would manage at her meeting with the school. He knew that she was still slightly fragile from her ordeal last year. But to see her now made him believe that she was far beyond the frail woman he pulled from the ghastly fire. "So I take it the meeting went well!" Mark teased as Holly unwound herself from his embrace. "Well?" She mocked. "It was absolutely great!" Holly fibbed in a slightly unsteady voice. "As a matter of fact Mariner High also has a new principle; Paul Murphy, who I met today as well." She explained. "Though I never found out what happened to the principle in charge when I was there last." She commented flopping down on the couch.

"That's great news Holly." Mark began. "And I've got some more good news." He began as he watched Holly remove her high heels and sit cross-legged on the couch. "Your sister and Rocky are coming over tonight for dinner!" He expressed with a laugh. "What?!" Holly asked in shock. She hadn't seen Mileena in weeks. "Your kidding right?" She asked jumping up from the couch excited. "Nope. Not at all baby. They should be here in a little while and Rocky and I are cooking for you girls." He said with a broad smile that made Holly's heart quicken. "This is the best day Mark." Holly started as tears welled up in her eyes. "I don't know what I would do without you in my life." She exclaimed going to Mark again and leaning into his embrace. Mark held her silently. She was still childlike and insecure at times, but Mark had long since gotten used to it. Sometimes it actually brought out an inner strength in him that no woman had ever done to him before.

After dinner Ian and Paul walked outside to smoke a cigarette. "Well I guess it's back to the room." Paul began. Ian took a long hit of his cigarette then blew smoke rings out; one after the other. "I rented us a house to stay in while we finish business here. We move in next week." Ian stated flatly. Paul was relieved to hear that comment. He just couldn't see the two of them staying in a small hotel room for God knows how long. Ian was his best friend but that didn't mean he wanted to be attached to his hip twenty-four seven. "Here's the spare key." Ian stated tossing it to Paul. Paul caught it and started fishing in his pocket for his rental car key ring. "So how'd it go today Paul with your meeting with Jonas.....and Holly?" He asked irritably. Paul looked up sensing Ian's slightly annoyed tone and decided to tread lightly.

"Just as planned Ian. Holly starts work this Monday." Paul thought back to how uncomfortable Holly looked in Jonas's office. Beneath her beautiful exterior, Paul felt that Holly she was terribly vulnerable. It would not take long for him to have complete control over her. "Did you find out which classroom is hers?" Ian asked, but already knew the answer to his own question. Paul was extremely thorough and never needed any help from Ian. "Yes Ian." Paul answered irritatingly. Everything is in place." He stated firmly. Ian dropped his cigarette on the ground, while looking Paul over, and crushed it out with his boot. He wondered if Holly would have any influence over Paul. He trusted his best friend with his life, but in Ian's experiences with him, Paul could sometimes be a pushover with women. "Call her tonight Paul." Ian called out to Paul as he walked away and towards his car. Paul watched Ian get in his car and drive away. Glancing at his watch he noticed it was six-thirty and wondered if Holly and her husband were even home.

Mileena and Rocky sat across the table from Holly and Mark. Both couples were laughing and enjoying their after dinner drinks. "Holly I am so happy for you!" Mileena gushed raising her glass to her sister. "Thanks Mil. I just can't believe my good fortune." Holly admitted. Mark put his arm around Holly and gave her a reassuring hug. Rocky raised his glass high and proclaimed, "Here's to Holly and Mark's future. May the past stay buried where it belongs." Mileena's heart quickened knowing that all the people that surrounded this very table could be in great danger, if she did not speak up soon. The group raised their glasses and gently brought them together with a resounding "Here! Here!"

Their glasses clinked lightly together and reminded Holly of sleigh bells. "Another drink Mil?" Holly asked taking her sister's empty glass. As she rose to refill the empty glass the phone rang. Holly frowned and then walked steadily into the kitchen to answer the phone. "Hello?" She began as she poured her sister another drink. "Good evening Holly. This is Paul Murphy." Holly stopped mid pour and set the heavy bottle down gingerly onto the counter. "Hello Paul. What can I do for you?" She asked slightly annoyed. Mileena, who was talking to Rocky and Mark, now turned her attention to Holly in the kitchen noticing her sister's bothered expression. Her body became rigid wondering who was on the other line. "I just wanted to congratulate you for re-securing your position at Mariner High School and to tell you that I really look forward to working with you in the coming weeks." Holly didn't know quite how to answer. It wasn't normal for the principle to keep up such a communication with a teacher. "Well, that's very good of you Paul." Holly began as she glanced into the dining room and made eye contact with Mileena. Mileena immediately rose from her chair and walked towards Holly calling out, "Hey Holly! Come on! We're gonna make another toast!" She hollered out purposely. "I see you have company Holly." Paul continued smoothly. "I will not bother you anymore tonight. I will see you bright and early Monday morning." He ended sighing slightly. Chills ran up Holly's back and she gripped the phone a little tighter. "Yes, Monday morning. G'night." Holly finished quickly. "Who was that?" Mileena asked once Holly had hung up the phone, and continued pouring her drink. "Paul Murphy. He's the new principle at Mariner High." Holly answered curtly.

"Problems?" Mileena asked watching Holly busy herself with nothing in the kitchen. "No, not really. He just doesn't behave like a man in his position." She stated flatly. "Why is he hitting on you?" Mileena laughed and then quieted quickly seeing Holly's expression. "I'm not sure Mil. I may be reading him wrong but he's awfully interested in my return to work." Mileena's mind reeled back to the letter she received from Ian, and also the threatening call she received on her cell phone. Could Paul Murphy be in any way connected to Ian? "No more shop talk Holly." Mileena began hurriedly. "Tonight we celebrate!"

Imminent Furor

As Holly got dressed for her first day back to work, Mark stood in the doorway of their bedroom and watched his lovely wife transform herself from his bedroom goddess into a simple but undeniably beautiful Biology teacher. "You are way too hot to be a Biology teacher Holly." He began walking slowly towards Holly. "Keep your distance cowboy." She began with a slight giggle. "We both have to go to work and I need to keep my head straight. I'm really nervous Mark." She confessed. Mark stood behind Holly. Their images reflected in the vanity table mirror before them. "There's nothing to be nervous about Holly. You know the school and the other teachers well enough. The only thing that has changed is that you have a year of new students." He reassured Holly bending slightly and kissing her neck. "And a new principle." Holly thought worriedly. Chills shot up Holly's back from Mark's kisses and her hands immediately made their way into Mark's hair. He kissed her lightly and then stood behind her once again. "Come on now Holly." He began taking her hand and pulling her up from her vanity chair. "The day will be over before you know it and you will be back home with me safe and sound." He comforted. Holly nodded silently and walked with Mark out of their bedroom to begin their day.

Ian sat motionless in his car outside of Mariner High School; watching Paul leave his vehicle and walk steadily towards the school. It was early and none of the students had arrived yet. Ian watched as a few teachers also made their way into the parking lot. Some stood chatting with one another before going in. Holly had not arrived yet and Ian was eager to see what she looked like after all these years.

Paul had just about entered the school when he stopped and turned to focus his attention on a particularly attractive blonde who had skipped up behind him. Ian watched as Paul smiled broadly and took her hand in his; shaking it gently. The blonde seemed very animated and obviously taken with Paul's good looks. Suddenly a car pulled along next to Ian's and stopped. As Ian turned his attention to the car he noticed Holly grabbing a few items from her backseat and then exciting her vehicle. Ian was stunned. He remembered Holly being attractive, but she had grown into a beautiful woman. She walked confidently across the parking lot and toward where Paul was standing with the other teachers. Ian noticed Paul glance up from his conversation and viewed Paul's expression change from pleasant to beaming upon seeing Holly near him. This angered Ian. He would have a talk with Paul this evening and make it abundantly clear how Paul was to proceed with Holly; Paul's lonely heart played no factor in his plans. Ian started the engine and made his way quickly out of the parking lot before Paul had a chance to notice him.

As Paul was making light conversation with the gorgeous blonde English teacher he had waved to last week, he noticed Holly walking quickly toward him. He and Holly's eyes locked and Paul noticed that her walk slowed a bit. "Excuse me." Paul indicated as he walked away from the bubbly teacher and over to Holly. The young teacher, so enraptured with Paul, scowled and turned abruptly then walked away briskly and into the entrance of the school. Holly watched Paul advance upon her and slowed her forward motion a even more. She tried to pretend that Paul's interest did not concern her in the least, but silently she felt awkward and more like the young female students she was about to instruct this morning. "Good morning Holly." Paul greeted as he came to a stop in front of Holly. "Morning Paul." Holly answered as she made her way past Paul and towards the school. Paul turned and began walking with Holly as her steps quickened. "Do you have plans for lunch today Holly?" Holly couldn't believe this guy. She stopped short and turned to face him. "As a matter of fact I do Paul. Mark is picking me up for lunch today." Holly lied, but she also hoped that her answer would put an end to Paul's more than obvious interest. "And also." She stated now more boldly. "My husband and I will be having lunch every day together." Paul was taken back slightly by Holly's boldness, but not undeterred. "How lovely for the two of you Holly." He began with a softer tone. The same tone Holly noticed in Jonas Seering's office last week. "I wish that I had a special someone to share my lunches with." He commented looking towards the ground. "So he's not married." Holly thought sadly. "Maybe that was the reason for his behavior the other day. He's probably just lonely." Holly suddenly felt bad for Paul. He was a new principle in a new school and obviously feeling quite alone. He had to feel somewhat out of place and probably just wanted some company. "Well, okay Paul. How about lunch tomorrow?" Holly asked suddenly feeling compelled to join him; for what otherwise would be a lonely lunchtime for Paul. Paul raised his head suddenly. A wide smile formed that completely lit up his face and made his eyes dance with happiness. "Are you sure your husband won't mind Holly?" He asked sheepishly, but still smiling. "Maybe Paul was just a kind man, who was putting on a brave face the other day" Holly thought to herself. "No, he won't mind Paul."

Holly and Mark hadn't made plans at all. Mark wouldn't have the time to meet Holly for lunch today or any other day. It just wasn't plausible in Mark's line of work. He was an on-call construction contractor. "Well then!" Paul began in a brighter tone. "I look forward to having lunch with you tomorrow Holly." Paul stated nearing her slightly. He was so close to her that she could detect his cologne and smell his aftershave lotion. Holly backed up awkwardly a step and without another word turned and walked into the school heading towards her classroom.

Mark abruptly slammed on the breaks and sat looking out the front window of his truck; utterly astonished by all that he saw. There in front of him stood

Trevor Morgan's old farm house! Just recently Mark had witnessed the beginnings of a home's construction process but this was the end result! It was like nothing had ever happened to Trevor's home. No raging fire, no pile of rubble and ashes, and until recently, no empty lot. Mark hastily cut the engine and jumped out of his truck. It had only been several weeks since he had driven by this area and had made eye contact with the dark stranger. The house then was merely a foundation and tons of building supplies and workers. Even in today's building standards a home such as Trevor's historic farmhouse would have taken far longer to finalize. Now as Mark stood next to his truck he saw before him an exact replica of Trevor Morgan's home. It was built with all new supplies of course, but everything was exactly the same! Prickly heat ran all over Mark's body as he neared the home that had once almost taken Holly's life.

Mark's throat was dry and his stomach churned violently. He walked slowly towards the house, hearing the screams of the past, the wails of the fire engines nearing, and Holly gasping for breath and pleading with him to save her. Mark's mind spun and he shook his head briskly to clear the thoughts that normally plagued Holly. As he reached the front steps his mind flashed to Mileena's face as she turned screaming at him, "Mark I've found Holly! She's in here!" On wobbly legs, Mark neared the tiny basement window and knelt down to the ground to have a look inside. He was utterly flabbergasted by what he saw. Sunlight. "What the?" Mark asked out loud continuing to peer into the window. No dark, smoke-filled basement. No pleas from Holly.

Just bright unadulterated sunlight streaming from.......
inside the house? Getting gingerly to his feet, Mark
walked quickly up the front porch stairs and directly
to the front door. Slowly he reached out his hand and
twisted the doorknob. The door opened effortlessly to
a complete wash of the same bright sunlight that he
saw through the tiny basement window. Dumbfounded
and a bit dazed Mark walked into the home, and was at
the very same time, in the backyard? He looked down
at his feet to discover that he was standing on grass?!
Shaky and ever so slowly, Mark turned around and was
beside himself with amazement by what he was now
seeing. The house was a facade! Not really a home at
all but a mere billboard of Trevor's home. Mark's knees
buckled and he found himself sitting down hard on the
ground; his head swimming with the many thoughts
that invaded his mind.

"Why would someone go to the trouble of building
a fake house?" He thought dizzily. "Everyone in this
county and most likely the state knew the story of this
house!" He ranted getting to his feet and shaking his
head once again. "Someone is obviously going to a lot
of trouble to bring a nightmare back into Holly's life!
And what of that dark stranger?" Mark continued to
question aloud, pondering the motives of an apparently
twisted individual. What was his connection to all
of this? Mark had a few friends at City Hall that he
would be able to gain some insight from. Once that
information was obtained, Mark would get to the
bottom of this!

As Holly left school and from her first official day
back teaching, she felt like she was on cloud nine! It

was as if she never left. No one questioned her absence, not even the nosiest of teachers there, and her new students were happy, enthusiastic, and quick to learn what she was teaching them. It was a dream that Holly definitely did not want to be awoken from. Once to her car, Holly loaded her bags and class lessons into her trunk and then entered her car. After starting the engine she noticed that a small piece of folded paper was stuck under her windshield wiper. Getting back out of her car Holly couldn't help but think that the whole nightmare with Trevor had started with a small note left on her apartment doorstep. She also noticed that it was beginning to rain a little heavier as tiny, cool drops landed on her bare arms. She remembered that Mark had cautioned her that morning that their area was due for a good storm. Holly stood silently and read the small note. "I look forward to lunch tomorrow with you Holly. I will meet you in the parking lot at one o'clock." Holly crumpled up the note and tossed it over her shoulder. Holly and Paul had already discussed earlier that day a meeting time and place, so this note was rather silly. But Holly did think it was rather sweet. Paul was obviously forlorn and looking for some company.

She got back into her vehicle and headed blissfully home; anxious to see Mark and tell him all about her first day back to work. And as she maneuvered her vehicle out of the parking lot and onto the highway that would lead her home, the heavily laden clouds above her opened up and gave to the earth their deserved sustenance.

Mark arrived home before Holly and made a beeline into the house while the rain came down in buckets.

Lightning flashed brightly and thunder boomed overhead; like the heavy footfalls of a dinosaur. Mark figured that the predicted storms were now heading here quickly and would be staying for a spell. Once inside the house and after he quickly yanked off his jacket, Mark noticed Holly pulling quickly into the driveway. Swiftly, Mark opened the hall closet and placed the heavy file folder from City Hall upon the shelf above the jackets. He then grabbed an umbrella and bolted out the front door to assist in Holly's arrival home. "Don't get out yet!" Mark hollered as he ran out the front door and over to Holly who was just exiting her car. "I got ya covered!" He exclaimed reaching her. "That is so sweet!" Holly giggled. "We have to get my things out of the trunk too!" She indicated as the two made their way to the rear of the car. Mark's mind was filled with the possibilities of what the City Hall folder, now hastily shoved into the hall closet, may contain. He hoped that the information would lead him to the crack pot who's bright idea it was to erect a facade exactly the same as Trevor Morgan's home. He knew one thing for sure though. This time no one would hurt Holly.

Ian sat silently waiting for Paul to get in for the night. The rain beat hard upon the hotel roof and lightning flickered off and on through the room's opaque curtains. It reminded Ian of the many neon lights of the city. Ian was now more than eager to inquire how the process was going with Holly. Ian knew that he was certainly holding up his end of the bargain both financially and literally. Ian's expression darkened slightly as he remembered the look on Paul's face this morning when he saw Holly walking up to him at the High School. There was absolutely no mistaking that Paul Murphy was a bit more than delighted to see her. That would have to stop. There was a big difference, in Ian's mind, between genuine happiness and faux happiness. Paul exuded genuine happiness. And that was not good. Paul had a job to do and Ian was paying him handsomely to complete this task. Not get all wound up and distracted. In all honestly, Holly would not be around for him to pursue after the job was complete anyway. Ian knew now that he would have to keep tabs on Paul until he was absolutely certain that Paul could control his natural instincts.

Lightning flashed brightly and thunder roared as the storm unleashed itself outside the windows of Holly and Mark's bedroom. Mark slept on peacefully as if there were utter silence in his surroundings. Hours had passed since the two had gone to bed for the night. And since retiring, Holly hadn't been able to fall asleep. She attributed her situation to that of sheer nerves from her first day back to work and she was also still slightly bothered by the whole Paul thing.

Since the horrific fire at Trevor's house, Holly hadn't been able to trust her instincts, her emotions, or to make sound judgments. It had taken her months to even think clearly.

She worried that this relationship with Paul may in fact be one of those times when her judgment was considerably clouded. But what would be the harm in having lunch with him? Paul knew that Holly was happily married. And unless Paul was a complete moron with no sense of morality, Holly supposed that she really didn't have anything to worry about. Holly also fretted a little about Mark's behavior earlier that evening. He seemed rather preoccupied over dinner. Which wasn't like him. They had both gone through so much together. And he wasn't his usual attentive self either. But rather indicated to her that he brought some paperwork home from work and would be working on that in their home office for awhile. As sleep finally covered Holly she settled herself to the fact that everything was fine and that a good night's sleep would take care of her restless mind.

A few hours later Holly slept peacefully and after what seemed like hours of waiting for her to do so, Mark left their bed and returned to their office. He wasn't able to completely go through the file as Holly kept sticking her head in and inquiring if he needed anything. Bless her heart. She meant well but had bugged Mark to the point where he figured that the only way that he could study the City Hall file properly was to do it after she had gone to sleep. After entering the office Mark quietly walked to the desk and turned on a small lamp. The rain still pounded relentlessly outside the window as the storm battered their community. Sitting comfortably, Mark opened the file once again and after flipping through the pages he already viewed, came to the section that contained the building permit information. The company that initially petitioned for the permit was called Brownstone Properties in New York City.

"Why would a company from New York City want to build here in Michigan? And not just build a normal dwelling but erect a facade of a building that had previously burnt to the ground?" Mark questioned perplexed. Further down the petition there indicated the pertinent contact information for their main office. Mark promptly wrote down the contact number on a post it note, and shoved it hastily into his wallet. He would make it a point to contact this company in the morning after returning the file to his friends at City Hall.

Paul worked silently and steadily in Holly's classroom and in barely enough light to see, as the night drew on. It was Ian's intention for him to start his tasks here where Holly would be spending a good deal of her day. Her home would come later. Paul had to wait to start his projects until the school was completely cleared out for the day and the janitors had finally gone home for the evening. It was now was one o'clock in the morning and Paul was growing weary from yet another full day of Ian's plans. Paul was also dealing with the nagging and annoying feelings that he was developing for Holly. This had never happened to him before. Paul had dealt with many a beautiful woman that Ian felt deserved his special treatments. Holly was different though. And Paul hadn't a clue as to why he couldn't shake her. Finishing his duties for the night, Paul stuffed the small flashlight into his briefcase and was preparing to head home when his cell phone rang. Looking at the illuminated face he noticed Ian's number glaring back at him. "Paul Murphy." Paul barked into the phone. "Either you are very thorough or you are wasting my very valuable time Paul. Which is it?" Ian demanded. Paul gripped the cell phone tightly in his hand and tried not to explode.

"I can assure you." He stated through gritted teeth. "That the time that it is taking me to prepare for **your** plans Ian are not wasted hours." Paul finished then abruptly snapped his cell phone shut.

Ian looked at his dead cell phone with simmering anger. "Do not mess with me old friend. This job will be done either with you or without you. That I can promise you."

The next afternoon Holly sat quietly behind her desk in the classroom and watched as her students took a small pop quiz that she had just issued them.

They all began scribbling their answers down quickly, while the wall clock ticked away by the classroom door. Holly wanted to see if they were getting a good grasp on the recent chapter that they were going over about the respiratory system. "Ten more minutes." Holly cautioned softly. She didn't want to bark out that pertinent information and disturb their concentration, but she felt that they needed to know that their precious twenty minutes was fading fast. One by one the students finished and walked up to the front of the classroom to hand Holly their assignment; they were then allowed to leave for the day. Glancing at the wall clock again Holly began to gather her things together for the drive home that afternoon. She reached down next to her and pulled open a large drawer where she kept her students assignments for the next day. But instead of the assignment folder she saw a picture laying in the bottom of the drawer. Frowning, Holly slowly lifted the picture out of the door and stopped short. Her hand began to shake and her mind spun at she viewed the image of Trevor staring back at her. "Where did this come from!" She yelled. Several students looked up with a start hearing their teacher's loud comment break the silence. Holly rose to her feet still shaking. The image of Trevor was not a favorable one by any stretch of the imagination. He was glaring at whoever took the picture of him and his eyes looked wild and menacing. Right then and there, Holly was back in the house with him and he was looming over her before another attack. Suddenly the brutal images from the fire came roaring back into Holly's mind. She saw the eerie dark basement, could feel the cold cement below her bruised and battered naked body, and could smell the smoke from the fire that was quickly engulfing the house that she was kept prisoner in. "Mrs. Harris? Are you okay?" One of the students asked upon seeing Holly begin to lose her composure. Holly couldn't answer. She felt as if she were struck by the very same lightning that flashed outside the classroom windows. Holly shook her head vigorously and tried to keep her emotions in check. "Class is dismissed early. Please go home!" Holly quickly pleaded sitting down hard in her chair; not being able to take her eyes off the image of Trevor that she held in her hand. All of her students exchanged quick looks and swiftly left their desks and headed for the classroom door. Holly set the picture down as she shook from head to toe. "How did this picture get in my desk?" She said out loud as tears welled up in her eyes. "Will I ever be rid of him!?" She cried out losing her self-control. She rose unsteadily and walked over to the bank of windows that lined one side of the classroom. The storm from last night was still here and was beginning to grow stronger. It was now accompanied with very high winds and hail. Holly looked desperately around her now unfamiliar and rapidly shifting classroom, noticing that several students had left their assignments on their desks.

Holly walked unsteadily over to one of the desks and with blurry eyes, clumsily grasped the back of the nearest chair to steady herself. She then retrieved the assignment for the student to finish tomorrow. All of a sudden Holly heard the far off sounds of sirens from an approaching fire truck. "Oh God!" Holly shrieked. "I've got to get out of here! The house is on fire!" She screamed believing that she was back in Trevor's basement and fighting for her life. Paul, who had been watching Holly's emotions come undone for several minutes now, ran into the classroom and grabbed Holly by the arms. "Holly? What's wrong?" He barked shaking her gently in an attempt to jar her senses back to her senses. Wildly, Holly looked into Paul's face and she was stunned with the realization that she was not in Trevor's basement but merely in her classroom and that there was, in fact, no fire. "Oh my God Paul!" Holly sobbed. "I...I don't know what happened." She whined and began to stagger slightly.. Paul steered her towards the nearest desk and assisted her into the seat. "I was starting to get ready to go home and I found a picture of Trevor in my desk drawer!" She began sobbing. "Who would put a picture of my ex-husband in my desk?" She whined putting her head into her hands. Paul quickly walked over to her desk and upon finding the picture that he had so recently placed in Holly's desk drawer, snatched it quickly and shoved it hastily into his pants pocket. "Where did you say the picture was Holly?"

Paul asked acting as if he were still searching for the picture. Holly looked up from her trembling hands and blinked several times to clear her vision. "It's.....it's right there Paul! I left it by my appointment blotter!" She cried. Paul continued his act of moving things around on Holly's desk and looking as if he were absolutely confused.

"Holly there is no picture here." He stated standing then and facing her squarely. Holly sat shocked and dismayed knowing that she had that picture in her hand just moments ago. She rose wearily to her feet and walked cautiously over to her desk as if half expecting something horrific to pop up from one of the drawers. Holly rounded her desk and stood next to Paul. Her dark brown eyes frantically searched the top on her desk for Trevor's picture. "What's happening?" She whispered in a child-like voice. "Holly are you alright?" Paul asked turning her to face him. She looked quite like a child who had just awoken from one of the worst nightmare imaginable. Her eyes were wide and filled with tears and her whole body vibrated with genuine terror. Paul felt a pang of guilt as he viewed the end result of his very own doing but fought against himself and kept his chin firm for Ian. Holly couldn't have possibly murdered Ian's brother Trevor. To Paul, Holly just did not appear to have that trait in her. She was too sweet, caring and obviously fragile. If anything, it was Trevor who had been the culprit of his own death. Paul drew Holly into his arms and held her tightly. Her small frame clung to him as she sobbed into his chest. "Shhh...it's okay Holly." Paul soothed gently as he stroked her long brown hair. "We'll figure out what's going on here okay?" He stated with genuine concern.

Mark sat in his truck and placed a call to Brownstone Properties in New York City. He was literally tormented by what he had seen the other day, on the property of what used to be Trevor's home. Mark wanted answers and he wanted them now. "God what if Holly by chance were to drive by that thing?" He thought wearily. "She would lose it." He assumed correctly but not knowing that Holly was already dealing with a slight emotional meltdown.

"Brownstone Properties." A disinterested woman's voice began. "Yes. Good Morning." Mark began. "I'm calling from Michigan and I am interested to know about a building project that was recently finished here by your company." He ended. "What is it that you want to know?" The woman responded quickly. "I'm inquiring as to who the people are that are responsible for this project!" Mark responded slightly annoyed. "One moment." She mumbled and immediately put Mark on hold. After several minutes the woman returned to the call. "The owners are out of state. Can I have them return your call?" She asked impatiently. Mark sighed heavily hoping that he could get this done quickly without Holly finding out. It was something that he wanted to distance his wife from, if at all possible. "Yes, my name is Mark Harris. Could you please have one of your bosses call me back?" He questioned then gave the curt receptionist his cell phone number and ended the call abruptly. Mark decided then that it was time to head home and get out of the increasingly nasty weather. Holly would be home in a few hours and they were planning to go to dinner tonight. But before heading off, Mark wanted one more look at the property that was really getting under his skin and could potentially destroy his wife's already fragile existence

An hour later Ian stood rigidly outside of his hotel room smoking a cigarette. He listened intently to his voice mail and became livid at the message he received. "So Mr. Harris is nosing into my affairs." He thought. Ian advanced immediately to his car and swiftly got inside and out of the storm. Ian knew long ago, that Mark Harris would be a major factor in his plans and that he would eventually have to deal with it. And now seemed as good a time as any to address this.

And Ian still had his doubts about Paul's recent behavior with Holly, but laid them aside until he finished his end of the business with Mark. On the seat next to Ian lay his brief case and another black bag, but before pulling away from the hotel Ian inspected the contents methodically.

"Are you feeling better now Holly?" Paul asked as he helped Holly onto her living room couch and handed her a cup of hot coffee he just prepared. "Yes, thank you Paul." She began as she took the cup into her trembling hands. "I'm so embarrassed and I really don't know what to say." She began. "I thought that I had a handle on the whole Trevor incident a long time ago." She confessed taking a sip of her coffee. Paul was still standing and looking around Holly and Mark's living room. It was cozy and inviting. "I thank you for following me home Paul. I'm not sure if I could have made it here on my own." Paul turned and locked eyes with Holly. She appeared to be very much younger than her age of twenty six. She was curled up with her feet tucked under her and a small throw blanket draped over her legs. Paul again felt an inner stirring that he wished was not taking place. "That's not a problem Holly. It's my job to make sure that my staff is happy and secure." He sheepishly replied and being very aware of how ridiculous his response sounded. Holly didn't know about the happy part but she was beginning to feel a sense of security around Paul Murphy. "I also had selfish reasons for following you home." Paul began as he walked over to the couch and sat down. "You are a good teacher Holly. I've seen you interact with your students. I want you to be an integral part of their academic lives." He stated emphatically but meaning otherwise.

"Thank you Paul, but judging by the looks on some of their faces this afternoon I wouldn't be surprised if they thought that I was the crazy." Holly commented laughing. Lightning suddenly lit up the whole living room followed immediately by a piercing crack of thunder. Holly jumped up off the couch and looked around startled. "Damn that was close!" She exclaimed wondering then what in the world was keeping Mark. It was almost five o'clock and he usually beat her home. She walked over to the front windows and watched the rain pound the front yard and driveway. You could barely see across the road. "I should be going now Holly." Paul began reluctantly grabbing his coat. "Oh." Holly replied turning and watching as he put on his coat. "Well, thank you again Paul." She stated wearily watching Paul slip on his overcoat "I will see you bright and early tomorrow morning." He began.

"And I'll leave my business card here on the table if you need anything Holly." He stated placing the business card on the foyer table and walking out the front door. Holly was exhausted and decided that she would take a quick shower and maybe lay down on the couch for a short nap before Mark arrived home. She walked slowly into the bathroom and stood looking in the mirror. Her appearance was strained and disheveled; her eyes swollen and red. Holly quickly undressed and stepped into the shower letting the hot water massage her tired body. "What is going on here?" She asked herself. "I know that Trevor is dead and gone so how did his picture end up in my desk?" She mused as she gingerly washed her hair. "Someone is playing games with me, but who? Who would knowingly try to hurt me?" Holly questioned as she rinsed off and exited the shower. Her body felt so heavy and her head was growing tired from the afternoon's event.

She decided then that a quick nap on the couch before Mark got home was just the medicine she required.

Mark parked his truck on the muddy dirt driveway and got out of the vehicle. His heavy boots sank deeply into the inundated earth. He quickly yanked his hood up over his head to shield himself from the downpour and the brisk wind that accompanied it. There in front of him stood silently the manifestation of what was once Trevor's home. Mark shuddered slightly and drew his coat together tighter in front of him. He completely understood now that the nightmarish home of his and Holly's horrid memories, no longer existed. But standing as he was in front of this simulation, it was hard to differentiate between the two. The workmanship was astounding. Whoever was responsible for this duplication was an artist. And seeing it for the second time in as many days, Mark was still beside himself with a feeling of dread. This time however Mark did not need to "enter" the house by way of the front door. He walked around the monstrous ruse and was again in the yard behind it. All in all the "home" was only about eight feet thick but to be facing it, one would wonder about all the rooms inside and just who occupied it. It was, in Mark's mind, a mind-blowing exploit. The rain was soaking him to the bone and Mark knew that he would have to wait until he heard back from Brownstone Properties to get any further information. Scowling, he gathered his coat against him and prepared for the drive home. But as Mark turned to leave the dark stranger stood facing him; silent and menacing. He wore the same dark trench coat and hat that Mark had seen before; his face slightly shadowed by the brim.

Mark stopped short, bewildered, and immediately recognizing the man from the other day who's intense stare left him uneasy. And here he was plain as day and looking very daunting and unwavering. "How do you like my masterpiece Mark!?" He bellowed over the pounding rain. Mark physically blanched with the realization that this man not only knew his name, but was actually taking credit for this monstrosity. "Who the hell are you!?" Mark yelled back pulling his jacket even tighter against him as the wind lashed his face. The man in the dark trench coat grinned sadistically and started to walk slowly toward Mark. Lightning flicked and flashed vividly overhead and thunder cracked and then roared in Mark's ears and rumbled below his feet. The storm was at its peak and Mark now wished that his curiosity this afternoon wouldn't have gotten the better of him. The dark stranger stood before Mark and removed his hat, then bowed ridiculously as if they were meeting at a diplomatic affair. Standing tall again he remarked emphatically, "Allow me to introduce myself to you." He began. "I am Ian Morgan." At first Mark didn't find his name to be that remarkable until, like the lightning that cracked and flashed around him, the dawn came. "Ian Morgan!!? Mark choked stumbling backwards literally astounded. "Trevor Morgan's brother??" He questioned slipping on the thick mud below his feet. Mark could not believe this was happening. Another evil Morgan sibling now stood menacingly in front of him and Mark understood, with his whole being, just what the dark's stranger's intentions were now. "You're a nosy bastard Mark." Ian began unflinching. "I don't like people interfering in my personal business"

Mark quickly caught hold of the soaked facade as his feet began to slip and slide out from beneath him. The hammering rain came down in heavy sheets and made small streams all around the men. "Holly is not your personal business Ian!!" Mark growled between his teeth. "She is my wife and if you attempt to hurt her you will be sorry asshole." Ian threw back his head and roared with laughter then promptly pulled out a gun from his trench coat and shot Mark twice.

Paul drove like a madman through the seemingly relentless rain; heading back to Holly's house. After leaving her only momentarily, Paul received a text message from Ian simply stating, "Mark Harris has been removed." Paul knew that it would not be long before Holly would be next on Ian's list. And either he or Ian would be accomplishing that task. Paul could not, and would not, complete this job for Ian. There didn't seem to be any reason in his mind what so ever for ever hurting Holly. Paul knew that he would have to get Holly out of here before Ian got wind of his intentions.

Holly paced her living room with worry. Mark was very late and night had long fallen. The storm outside had not let up and in fact only promised to get worse and last throughout the night. She had tried several times to call Mark's cell phone to no avail. Holly knew that something was dreadfully wrong. She decided that she would venture out into the night and look for Mark herself. His truck may have broken down and that he may need assistance, but she also prayed silently and with all of her heart that nothing seriously happened to her husband, her soul mate. Holly quickly walked to the front coat closet and yanked her jacket from the hanger. Unexpectedly, something fell from the shelf above the coats as she was about to close the door behind her.

There on the closet floor lay a file folder; the contents scattered all over.

Holly knelt quickly and scooped up the folder and the separated papers, and carried them into the living room with her. She had never seen this folder before and she wondered how it had come to be placed in the coat closet.

After sitting on the couch and putting the file back together, Holly noticed the first page from the folder had a business name of Brownstone Properties and just below it the title, "Notice of intent to build". Holly frowned as she had never heard of that particular company before and wondered if this was something that Mark was working on for one reason or another. They shared so much together that Holly silently wondered why Mark had never mentioned this company to her before, and why he had hidden this information in the hall closet. Holly began swiftly thumbing through the extraneous pages until she came to the petitioner's business information. Apparently the company, Brownstone Properties, was located in New York City. Nothing odd about that jumped out at her, but further down the page was a sign off section listing the company's owners. A small cry escaped Holly's throat as she read aloud the two names listed, "Ian Morgan and Paul Murphy!" Holly jumped to her feet letting the papers in her hands flutter and fall to the floor. Her mind was spinning with information. "Ian Morgan?!? Trevor's brother?!?" She screamed out loud. And then yet another harsh realization. "My God! Paul Murphy knows Ian?" Her mind began filling with images and information. She saw Jonas Seering, the assistant principle of her high school, sitting behind his desk the morning of the meeting. "This is the new principle Holly, Paul Murphy." Holly saw herself greet Paul assuming that he was indeed the new principle. Holly felt her stomach heave.

The images shifted and she saw Paul consoling her in her classroom and then here at the house tonight after she found the picture of Trevor in her desk drawer! "Paul put it there!" She screamed. "He's working for Ian!" The information was too great for Holly to bear. She had come this far thinking that now with Trevor dead and gone she could finally come to terms with the fire and get on with her life. Now Ian was here to apparently take the place of his dead brother and he had with him Paul Murphy to help him with whatever sinister plans he had for her. Holly sobbed as she grabbed her cell phone and tried once again to call Mark. Something had happened to him, this she knew. And she also knew that Ian and Paul had something to do with it. As Holly waited for Mark's voice mail, she noticed Paul's car roaring up into her driveway. Holly dropped her cell phone and immediately ran to her bedroom, slamming the door behind her. She frantically scanned the room for some type of weapon that she could use against Paul should he be able to get into the house. She heard him yelling as he stood on the front porch. "Holly! Open the door! We have to talk!" Holly peeked out her bedroom window that faced the front yard. Paul stood silently on the porch with his hands shoved deep into his jacket pockets. "Go......away." She whispered sobbing. "Holly please!" Paul continued as he pounded on the door. "You and I are not safe anymore! Ian will kill us both if he finds us here!" Holly backed quickly away from the front windows and then ran back down the hall and quickly into the kitchen. Hoisting herself up onto the kitchen counter, she slid the kitchen window aside and began pushing on the screen to free it from the frame. Cold rain pelted her face and wetted the counter below her.

"Come on damnit! Move!" Holly yelled at the stiff and unyielding screen. Holly knew that if she could get out the kitchen window and into the back yard she could get to the garage which housed an old car that she and Mark kept for emergency situations. Night had long fallen and the backyard was as black as the ace of spades. Holly didn't hear Paul's loud voice nor did she hear his pounding on the front door anymore, as her feet reached the slippery wet ground below her. She hoped beyond hope that Paul had given up trying to convince her of something that Holly would not hear of. Slowly and shakily she began her short dark trek across the black backyard. The only light to be seen came from the streetlights behind her and they were over thirty feet away; allowing only slight allumination for cars to navigate with. Upon reaching the side door, Holly tried the knob and found it to be locked. She cursed in the clammy night air and knew that she wouldn't dare try to open the old garage door. She couldn't chance it. Holly made her way around to the back of the garage where she discovered two small windows above her head. They were wide open and contained no screens. "Why lock a door and have open windows?" Holly whispered aloud. But she was thankful for the blessing nevertheless. Reaching above her, Holly was just barely able to close her hands over the frame of the window and begin to pull herself up. Holly never had the strongest of arms and this little pull-up burned the muscles immediately in her biceps. She gritted her teeth against the burning in her arms and the cold hard metal cutting into the palms of her hands, when suddenly she was grasped around the waist and yanked back down to her feet. Holly struggled wildly against Paul's forceful grip around her waist, but to no avail.

"Holly stop!" Paul yelled over the din of the storm. "I'm here to help you please!"

He cried trying to get ahold of Holly who fought him like an alley cat. "Let me go you bastard!" Holly screamed beating Paul's chest with her fists. "I know all about you and Ian Morgan!" She wailed now kicking Paul with her free legs. Immediately she was put on the rain soaked ground as Paul straddled her body, pinning her weakened arms down with his. "Get off me!" Holly screamed trying valiantly to free herself. The pouring rain drenched her face and soaked her hair. Paul had no idea how Holly had found out about him and Ian, but that at least gave him a starting point with Holly. "Listen to me Holly! I used to work for Ian but I don't anymore!" He hollared over the driving wind and rain. "Right!" Holly began. "You lied to me Paul. You said that you were the new priciple of the school! Now I find out that you are working with Ian! Trevor's brother!" She cried wildly kicking Paul's back with her knees. Paul had to think quickly. He hadn't answered two of Ian's calls tonight and he knew that it would only be a matter of time before Ian would come on the run looking for him and for Holly "Holly you have to listen to me now!" Paul began with his face very close to hers. "We are both in grave danger. Me, because I betrayed Ian and didn't follow his plans, and you because......well, because you **are** Ian's plans." He finished slightly out of breath. Holly quieted knowing that her beloved Mark was also in Ian's plans. "And Mark!? Where is my husband?!" She screamed at Paul now sobbing uncontrollably. Paul grabbed Holly's arms even tighter. "Mark is gone Holly. Ian killed him." Holly looked into Paul's eyes and knew that he was telling the truth. She broke down as painful sobs tore painfully from her throat over the loss of her husband and her very best friend.

Mark was all Holly ever needed and loved, and now he was gone. And with him Holly's soul. She would never see his smiling face again, hear his soothing voice in her ear, or his loving touch upon her skin. Paul suddenly lifted Holly to her feet. "There is no time now for grieving Holly. We have to leave now." He stated firmly. Holly stared blankly at Paul not fully understanding his words. "Leave?" She questioned. "I can't just leave Paul! This is my home. And my sister is here too!" She sobbed uncontrollably. Paul shook Holly hard and hollered into her face. "If you do not go with me right now Holly you will be dead by morning!" He yelled over the wind and rain. "Ian will not stop until he finds us Holly. Do you understand me?" He questioned through gritted teeth. Paul would bind and gag Holly if he had to just to get her far away from the clutches of Ian Morgan's wrath. Ironically, Paul Murphy now found himself embroiled in rescuing a woman that he had intended to kill.

Ian's car came to a silent, rolling stop in front of Holly house. The rain had let up slightly, but the streets were still slick and teeming with tiny reflective streams that had not completely drained away. Ian sat incensed watching Paul and Holly run around inside her home obviously trying to gather as much "travel necessities" as they could anticipate needing. Ian could not believe the complete betrayal by his best and only friend. He had never in his life, and with all the people who had come and gone along with it, have ever imagined that Paul would be one of those people. Ian also noticed Paul's car sitting idle beside Holly's in the darkened driveway.

"I have to call Mileena!" Holly begged for the second time. "She's my sister Paul, and she will worry herself sick if I just up and leave." She stressed emphatically knowing in her heart that this would probably be the last time she spoke to Mileena for a very long time. "We have to leave NOW Holly! How many times must I tell you this?!" Paul yelled. "If you need to call Mileena you will have to do so on the way to the airport." Paul ended without waiting for a reply from Holly. Holly watched as Paul walked briskly into her kitchen; yanking open drawers and cupboards while he searched for necessities that they would need. "Airport!?" Holly yelled bewildered. "Are we leaving town?" She asked as she watched Paul throw a handful of items into a large duffle bag and quickly stride up to her. He looked angry and a bit disheveled. Paul roughly grabbed Holly by the arm while glancing out the front living rooms windows, and then pulled her along with him into the kitchen. Paul was through with negotiating with Holly. Ian had been parked in front of the house for several minutes now and it would only be a matter of time before he made his move. Holly began crying again and resisting Paul's lead but he would have nothing of it as he roughly grabbed Holly around the waist and lifted her slightly. Holly fought back valiantly but to no avail as Paul roughly shoved her, once again, back through the kitchen window. Paul then threw the duffle bag after her and then made his own way through the window. Once out the window he again grabbed Holly by the arm and pulled her along with him and into the garage; all the while mindful that Ian had silently left his car and was now somewhere on the property.

"Paul where are we going?" Holly pleaded as they reached the back door of the garage.

Paul quietly opened the door and shoved Holly inside with him. "Where you will be safe Holly."

"I need to change my flight plans." Ian angrily stated then listened as the customer service person began keying information into the computer. "There is a charge for this service Mr. Morgan." She indicated as she continued to type. "I am aware of that! " Ian snapped as he kept an eye on Holly and Paul moving slowly into the garage. "I must leave immediately." He barked then glanced at his watch. It was almost dawn and Ian knew that he would probably not be able to get a decent flight out for several hours. Nor would Paul and Holly. "I have a flight departing out of Detroit's Metropolitan Airport at four forty-five and arriving at New York's La Guardia Airport at six fifteen" The woman suggested. "Fine, would you just book it for the love of God!" Ian bellowed as he slowly began moving towards the backyard. He saw a small light moving around inside the garage as Holly and Paul searched for the spare car keys that were hidden inside. The very same set that Ian obtained while the two scrambled around inside the house. Holly and Paul would be without transportation unless they braved the likes of Ian and took their own cars for their departure.

"There gone!" Holly cried out. "I swear to you Paul this is where Mark and I kept the keys to the spare car." She indicated glancing wildly around the area above the back door. She knew that Mark had a spare key for the car hidden just above the back door on a simple unfinished beam. Now there was nothing there but dust. Paul didn't know whether or not to believe Holly. He felt that this may be a trick of hers so that she could stay behind; not believing the full magnitude of Ian's wrath.

"Holly do not play games with me!" Paul growled approaching Holly in full stride. "I have warned you more times than I care to about Ian." Holly blanched and tried to move away from Paul's approach, but he was upon her before she could react further. Paul grabbed Holly by the arms and shook her hard. "If we do not find these keys right now Holly we will both be dead!" He breathed into her face. "FIND THEM!" He yelled pushing Holly against the back door. Holly landed against the door with a loud thud and she exhaled quickly the air from her lungs. Her mind was spinning with all that was happening around her and she knew that she had to escape to save her own life. Without another thought Holly quickly turned around, grabbed the door knob, and was out the door before Paul knew what was happening. "HOLLY!" Paul screamed knowing that Ian was not far from the garage and just waiting for one or both of them to emerge.

As Ian hung up the phone he saw Holly bolt from the garage and run full speed into the wet and blackened backyard. His hand immediately went into his trench coat pocket and wrap tightly around the cold steel of his revolver. Suddenly, Ian then spied Paul running from the garage and quickly following Holly. This was Ian's chance. If either of them were able to get to the airport before him, Ian knew that he would have a difficult time locating the two once they were in New York City. Paul was a master of those city streets and had eluded many "associates" in the past. Ian strode boldly up the driveway and into the direction that Holly and Paul had taken. They couldn't have gotten far. The backyard was completely bordered by a chain link fence and if either on of them began to climb it, Ian would be sure to hear them. But as he reached the darkest part of the yard he heard nothing.

No footfalls against the rain soaked earth and grass. No rustling of overcoats against clothes. Nothing. Ian stopped his pace and listened.

Holly sat high above Ian in a large, wet maple tree. She sat there nervously but quietly watching him angrily pace the dark backyard below her. Her next door neighbor's backyard security light blinked off and on with the detection of something in their backyard, and this afforded Holly the opportunity to keep somewhat of an eye on Ian. Holly's heart was beating so furiously in her chest that she was almost certain that he could hear it. And what of Paul? She hadn't seen him since she had ran from the garage and up into this trusty tree. The very same tree that was going to accommodate a tree house, that Mark had intended to build when they had kids. Holly knew Paul was close. She could feel him. And almost detect his cologne. As Holly adjusted herself to get a better view of Ian she began slipping against the tree limb's slippery surface. "God please don't let me fall!" She thought as she dug her fingernails into the wet bark and held on for dear life. But she was losing the battle as her feet slipped away from her and off the branch she slipped. Suddenly she was seized by two powerful hands and hauled up back onto the large branch. "Don't move!" Paul breathed into her face. "Don't make a sound Holly." Holly and Paul watched as Ian's head shot up in their direction. He stood menacingly bold as he fixed his icy stare upon them. "He can't see us." Paul whispered. "But he heard **you** for sure." He admonished tightening his grip on Holly's trembling body.

Ian heard the crack of a tree branch and turned quickly in its direction. He tried to focus his gaze on a large maple tree to the left of him and where the crack seemed to have originated from. But as blind as a bat in the utter pitch of the backyard, Ian could not tell if an animal was playing in the trees or Holly and Paul. He would find out though as he quickly fired off two shots into the direction of the noise.

Holly quickly sucked her breath in after the first initial blast of Ian's gun. Paul immediately covered Holly's body with his own and held on to her for dear life. Holly's ears were ringing and she was shaking uncontrollably with fear and utter dismay as immediately as the first, the second shot fired off. Several dogs in the neighborhood began barking hysterically and lights from the immediately surrounding homes came to life.

Holly heard a small thud somewhere near her and assumed the bullet from the second shot had lodged itself in the tree branch. Paul then leaned into to Holly. "I am going to throw something passed Ian and into another tree." He began in a hurried whisper. "Once I've done that you need to get out of this tree and run as fast as you can to my car Holly. Do you understand?" He asked quickly. Holly unwound herself from Paul's grip and sat staring wildly at his shadow. "We'll never make it Paul!" She whispered hotly.

"Ian is not that stupid! He'll hear us and shoot us!" She choked beginning to feel the fringes of anxiety. Paul then leaned back against the large trunk of the tree and steadied himself. "Noooo!" Holly whispered as she saw Paul take something from his jacket and prepare to launch it into the other tree.

Holly looked quickly below her and realized that she wasn't really that far off the ground. She then heard Paul whisper, "One........two........three."

As Ian was preparing to fire another round into the tree where Holly and Paul were, another large cracking sound was heard in the tree to the right of him. This had to be where they were. The loud break was obviously from the weight of either Holly or Paul. Ian strode quickly to the next tree and began firing his gun with reckless abandon.

At the first sound of the item flying by her, Holly jumped down from her safe branch; landing with a thud on her feet and not far behind Ian. Paul came directly behind her and grabbed her arm. They both ran as if the devil were on their heals until they ended up at the driveway and by Paul's car. "Get in Holly now!"

Paul whispered through gritted teeth. Once inside Paul quickly started the car and threw it into reverse. The cars tires slipped on the slick driveway and the car slid and swerved as Paul punched the gas and backed out of the driveway. "Holly get down!" Paul barked as the windshield began getting hit with bullets. Holly screamed and laid down on the riders side seat. The noise was absolutely deafening! Paul watched as Ian ran towards his car, gun in hand, firing feverishly towards the two of them. Once into the street, Paul slammed the gear into drive and took off like a shot down the slick street. He watched in his rearview mirror as Ian ran to his own vehicle and prepared to take off after them.

"My God Paul we're gonna die!" Holly screamed. Paul did not answer. He was too intent on getting them out of this neighborhood and onto a major highway. "Here." Paul stated as he handed Holly his cell phone. "Call your sister now and say good-bye. It's going to be a very long time until you are back this way again." Holly's head came up from the seat like a shot as she stared at the cell phone in Paul's hand, then toward his darkened profile. His gaze was fixed upon the road in front of him and he didn't bother to look Holly's way. He couldn't. Holly knew that he was deadly serious. Her beloved home, her treasured sister, and her husband and treasured soul mate Mark; who was now dead and gone; all were to be a memory to her now. But nothing prepared her for what she would soon encounter when she would find herself in Paul's world. Holly took the phone from Paul and began to dial her sister's number. "Be as brief as you can Holly. Ian has a GPS device on my cell phone. I will get rid of it once you've made your call." Paul instructed in an almost embarrassed tone. Holly glanced away from the phone briefly and stated, "Some friend." with obvious bitterness. After placing the call to her sister, Mileena answered on the second ring. "Mil? It's Holly. I don't have much time to talk and I don't have time to explain to you everything that has happened over the past few days, so please don't interrupt and just listen!" Holly rambled quickly and without allowing Mileena to respond she continued. Mark is dead and Trevor's brother Ian killed him as part of a revenge plot against me!" Holly chocked and sobbed. Mileena sat dumbfounded as her sister continued explaining to her that this would be their last call together for a very, very long time. "I love you Mil!" Holly choked. Paul gingerly reached over and snatched the phone from Holly's hand and tossed it out the driver's side window.

Ancillary World

"I need two one-way tickets to La Guardia Airport please." Paul asked in a hurried tone. He looked disheveled in a suit that he had worn for the past day and a half. Holly stood next to him dazed and a little more than confused. Her hair was messy, her makeup long washed away from tears, and her eyes were sticky and swollen. She simply could not wrap her head around all that had occurred to her in a matter of weeks. She felt angry, sad, paranoid, sick to her stomach and more than exhausted. It was very early in the morning and Detroit's Metropolitan Airport was not half as busy as most days. Most people who were waiting for flights, Holly noticed, were sleeping in their own makeshift accommodations. Some had sleeping bags and some just slung themselves across the unyielding terminal seats. A few passengers wandered around with coffee or talked on their cell phones while they waited. The calm surroundings made Holly all the more nervous knowing that Ian could spot the two of them that much easier. "I have a flight leaving in forty-five minutes sir."

The customer service person conveyed. Holly thought that would be an unbearable time for them to wait. "Do you have anything sooner?" She asked pushing Paul aside and flashing the woman a heartrending smile. "We have been through so much and we just want to go home." Paul was astonished at Holly readiness to leave her home. "Let me check." The attendant replied "Just one moment." Holly saw the rather humorous look on Paul's face and grew angry. "Let's get something straight right here and right now Paul." She began angrily. "I will never, ever forgive you for all that you have brought upon me and my family."

Paul stood wearily in front of Holly and allowed her to get everything off her chest. "Thanks to you and Ian my husband is dead and I might as well be too. And all because your psychopath friend thinks that I killed his lunatic brother!" Holly exclaimed growing louder and angrier with each word. "And if you think for one minute that I will not find my way back home one day you are sadly mistaken asshole!" She finished taking the tickets from the customer service person and standing boldly in front of Paul. Holly watched an array of emotions crossed Paul's darkened features. But his expression suddenly changed then from empathy to sheer alarm. "Holly run.......RUN!"

Ian's car flew into the airport parking lot and came to a screeching halt at the departure terminal's valet parking lane. Leaping out of his car Ian rounded to the back and opened the trunk quickly. "Can I park your car sir?" A young and less than enthusiastic man inquired. "I don't care what the fuck you do with it!" Ian barked grabbing his bag and slamming the trunk lid closed. The parking attendant jumped and slowly backed up a few paces to avoid Ian's obvious hot temper. "Here keep it!" Ian bellowed throwing the rental car keys to the timid young man as he raced passed him and into the terminal building. Once inside Ian's eyes darted about madly as he tried to locate his particular airline check-in desk. Finally locating it just a few yard ahead of him, Ian's steps quickened as he didn't have much time in order to retrieve his boarding pass for a flight that would be the same as Holly and Paul's. Theirs was due to depart in a matter of minutes. Out of breath and looking disheveled, Ian spoke quickly to the female attendant behind the desk.

Holly and Mark ran full speed, tickets in hand, towards their departure gate. Paul had spied Ian running into the terminal after them and he knew that they would be hard pressed to elude him if they didn't get a good head start. "What if he's able to get a seat on our flight?!" Holly yelled wildly as they ran together down a long corridor that connected the two sections of the airport. "We'll cross that bridge when we come to it Holly!" Paul barked maintaining his full run. Nearing their gate Holly noticed that passengers were all ready boarding. "Hurry Holly!" Paul remarked grabbing her arm. "I don't need your help!" Holly yelled back yanking her arm out of Paul's grip and running ahead of him. Holly and Paul fell in behind the last group of people in line to board. To Holly it seemed like an eternity before she and Paul were able to give the gate attendant their tickets and travel down through the long passageway that connected the terminal to the airplane. Holly turned quickly and glancing behind her to see the attendant slowly closing the departure door. "We're all the way to the back." Paul remarked as he glanced at his ticket. Holly stole a quick glance at her ticket confirming Paul's comment. "Hopefully someone will be sitting between us." She thought irritably.

Ian tapped his foot impatiently as the customer service person began printing out his boarding pass. Glancing openly at his watch he figured that he would have not even ten minutes to get to his gate. He also knew that Holly and Paul were probably already boarding, if not getting settled into their seats. "Enjoy your flight." The woman stated handing Ian his boarding pass. Ian immediately turned and took off towards his gate.

Holly glanced around quickly as she and Paul entered the airplane and walked down the narrow aisle towards their seats. The plane was almost full and in Holly's mind that was a very good thing. "Here we are." Paul commented as he slid into the section of three seats. "I want the window." Holly stated firmly as she stood in the aisle glaring at him. "Fine!" Paul shot back angrily sliding back across the seats and allowing Holly her window seat. "Not much to see this time of the night." He remarked as Holly moved past him and into her seat. Paul then took the seat next to her. "Don't like the aisle?" Holly mentioned without taking her attention from the window. Paul let the comment go and sat firmly in the middle seat. "Let's at least try to be civil to one another Holly. We are going to be spending a lot of time together from now on." Holly glanced at Paul noticing that he had laid his head back against the seat and closed his eyes. "Not if I have anything to say about it." She thought heatedly making short glances towards the front of the plane and taking stock of each and every passenger that boarded after her. No sign of Ian. And as the plane started slowly moving backwards, and the flight attendant slammed the outer door closed, Holly also leaned her head back against her seat, closed her eyes, and fell into a deep sleep.

As Ian boarded the plane he quickly searched each and every seat he passed for signs of Holly and Paul. And as he searched, the plane began moving backwards. Ian grabbed the seat head next to him for balance and continued to look for signs of the pair. "You need to take your seat now sir. We are preparing for take off." A flight attendant instructed. Ian glanced quickly at his ticket and then directly above him to the seating signs.

His seat was the next set back. Taking his seat quickly and scowling at the flight attendant, Ian fumed with his current situation. Holly and Paul would not elude him. This was their flight too and once the plane was in the air he would locate them and then make sure that they all left together. Ian flipped open his cell phone and began punching in an array of numbers and letters as he quickly text messaged his associates back home. If Holly and Paul happened to escape him this time Ian was certain that once they landed they wouldn't make it out of the terminal and into the city.

Holly's sleep was restless as she went in and out of dreams. And every one of them involved her beloved husband Mark. She saw them together and loving one another completely; never to be separated. In her dreams she was complete and at peace. Holly wept each time she awoke and realized that she was never going to see him again. Her body ached for him and her heart felt as though her whole life was now a mere memory. She was empty, and Ian and Paul had stolen her whole life away from her. Holly had no idea what lay ahead of her now. She knew that she was going to New York City and most likely to a town that Paul was familiar with. Holly had never been to a big city before. Even in her younger years when she lived in California she was far from a major city. "Holly!" Paul spoke hotly in her ear. "Wake up. Let's go!" Holly woke up startled and looked around wildly; wondering how long she had been asleep. "Are we hear already?" She asked sleepily as she glanced out the window noticing that they were still in line for take off and hadn't even left the tarmac yet!

"What's going on Paul?! Why haven't we left yet?" She asked dismayed. "Grab your bag now!"

Paul instructed as he grabbed Holly by the arm and pulled her to her feet. Several passengers turned to watch Holly and Paul hotly argue with one another as they left their seats. A large man moved into the aisle preventing the two from passing. "You okay Miss?" The man asked Holly noticing she was almost near tears again. "Stay out of it!" Paul barked. "My wife is very ill and we need to get off the plane." The man quickly moved aside as Paul pulled Holly along with him to the rear of the plane. "What is going on?" Holly whispered hotly to Paul as they neared a flight attendant waiting for them. "Trust me Holly. I'll explain everything once we are back in the airport." Holly reluctantly followed Paul to rear of the plane and then watched as the flight attendant quickly opened the door and lead them down the stairs and onto the tarmac. "Thank you." Paul said to the flight attendant who had a very worried look on her face. "You're welcome sir. I hope your wife feels better soon." She answered as she returned to the stairs and then returned quickly back into the plane. Paul stood for several minutes next to Holly and watched the plane finally begin to back up. "Paul what the hell is going on!?" Holly screamed over the deafening engines of the plane. Paul stood motionless as he watched the plane depart and one plane window in particular. Ian was glaring back at him from his seat inside the plane. The look Ian wore gave Paul a cold chill down his spine as he turned his focus to Holly. "Ian was on our flight Holly. We have to go back to the desk and secure another flight." Holly stood dumbfounded. She hadn't seen Ian on their flight. But apparently Paul had and took drastic measures to see that the two of them were able to leave the plane quickly. She was thankful for that. Paul not only saved her, but quite possibly a few hundred other people as well.

Four hours later Holly and Paul's plane landed at New York's La Guardia Airport. "Keep your eyes open Holly. Ian could be anywhere." Paul instructed as they left their seats and followed the other passengers departing the plane. Holly was a ball of nerves as she followed closely behind Paul. She noticed that Paul was talking softly but quickly to someone ahead of him in line, but she could not make out a word of what he was saying. The man looked back over Paul's shoulder suddenly and looked at Holly momentarily. The two men continued whispering to one another, then Paul turned back to Holly when the line slowed a bit. "Whatever you see, feel, or hear now Holly remember that I am doing this for your own good." Holly had no idea what Paul meant, but the look on his face made her blood run cold. She noticed that the strange man had also handed Paul a cell phone, which Paul directly shoved into his jacket pocket. "Did Paul know this man?" She thought wearily. Everything to Holly, since they had left the first plane, was a blur. She remembered they secured another flight and that Paul had excused himself from their seats after they had boarded. But Holly had fallen asleep after that and when she awoke they were already in New York City.

The line began to move more fluidly now and before Holly knew it, Paul had grabbed her arm and was quickly pulling her along the gangway and into the airport terminal. Paul also followed closely behind the strange man that he was talking to on the plane. "He must know that man." Holly thought nervously. "Apparently, Paul knows a lot of people." She reasoned despairingly. Suddenly out of nowhere a large trench coat was draped over her head and someone was lifting her into their arms. Holly struggled at first out of habit and human nature, but tried to remain calm as she headed Paul's words from the plane.

Holly's body shook and bobbed as the person carrying her ran with a heavy footed gate. She felt suffocated and began to panic despite her best efforts. A small whine escaped her throat as she was shifted from one set of arms to another. The coat smelled of cigarette smoke and aftershave. But not Paul's brand of aftershave. Suddenly she was heaved into the back seat of a vehicle and landed on her side against the cool unyielding seat. She heard many hushed voices around her and then the engine started. "Paul?" She cried out with sheer terror. "Where are you?" She screamed. A muffled voice was suddenly next to her head and above the coat. "Holly I'm right here." Paul stated flatly. "What's happening!? Where are we going!?" She cried trying to claw her way out from underneath the heavy coat. Paul placed his hand on the coat and pressed slightly letting Holly know that she was to stay put. He sighed openly and looked at Holly's coat-enveloped body. She was shaking from head to toe. His heart twisted knowing that she had been through so much and that he was responsible for at least three quarters, if not all of it. But he could not let her see the route to his place. In Paul's mind it was too risky. She may try to escape and make her way back to the airport. Then she would be at the mercy of Ian, who Paul knew now was at his own place and making further plans for the two of them. Paul also knew that New York City was a big place and one that Holly had never seen the likes of. One wrong turn for Holly down any number of the streets therein and she would be lost forever. Paul leaned back towards Holly then. "Try to get some sleep Holly. We'll be there soon." Holly sobbed openly as she brought her knees up into her chest; hugging herself against this horrible nightmare.

The car suddenly shifted and Holly grabbed the car seat to steady herself. She felt the vehicle increase its speed, moving very fast and weaving in and out of traffic. Her stomach lurched with the rollercoaster ride she was experiencing. She then felt Paul's hand upon her hip as he held her firmly in place. Holly quieted somewhat and Paul could hear her softly crying and calling out for Mark.

An hour later Holly awoke with a start and sat up quickly. Trembling from head to toe, she glanced from one end of a dark and tiny room to the next not recognizing her surroundings. A small lamp was on next to the couch and atop of a small end table that was littered with a full ashtray, an old coffee cup, and a few discarded items. Throwing the coat off of her, Holly noticed that she had been sleeping on a couch and that she was in a studio size apartment. Standing slowly and wearily she immediately became aware that she was alone and the apartment dead silent. Glancing down to a small coffee table in front of the couch, she noticed a piece of paper with her name at the top. Sitting back down gingerly, Holly grabbed the note and began to read. *"Holly. Gone to get some food. Be back shortly. Paul."* Holly let the note slip from her fingers as she rose again and began walking slowly around the meager surroundings. To her left was a bank of heavily draped windows and as she neared them she noticed a light from behind the drapes. Pulling them aside she was struck first with the revelation that she was several floors up from the ground. Six to be exact. The windows themselves were almost amber colored from smoke stain and neglect. The building directly across the street had exactly the same amount of floors from what she could see, and Holly could only assume that her building was in the same rundown condition as the one she stood looking at.

Glancing to the ground below she watched a myriad of activity. Many cars, trucks, taxis, and an enormous amount of people milled about in every direction. It had rained while she slept and the streets seemed mirror-like and perfectly reflected the hustle and bustle. Holly tried valiantly to open the window and allow some fresh air to permeate the damp and musty room but the windows were long ago painted shut and refused to budge. "Lovely." She muttered aloud. "Get away from the windows now!" Holly jumped and spun around to see Paul standing in the middle of the room. She hadn't even heard him come in. His look was menacing and his arms were laden with bags of groceries. His coat was damp and disheveled. "God Paul!" Holly shrieked trembling from head to toe. "You don't have to yell at me!" She hollered. Holly's nerves were shot and it wouldn't take much to send her into a tailspin. She watched as Paul moved into the kitchen area and set the bags upon a small table. He didn't answer Holly merely set about unloading the bags. "Is this your apartment?" Holly inquired with obvious distaste. Paul stopped briefly then continued his task. "No." He replied without further explanation as to why he chose to bring Holly to this dump. Holly would not be swayed by Paul's rudeness. She slowly approached the table glancing at his selection of groceries. All the necessities a "man" would need for a long stay that was for sure. Cigarettes, beer, chips, and an array of snack food littered the table. "Why aren't we staying at your place then?" Holly asked as she spotted a nice bottle of wine. "You really can't be that damn naive Holly!" Paul barked glaring at Holly. "Do you honestly believe that my apartment would not be the first place Ian would look for us?" He roared tossing the last bag of groceries to his feet.

Holly backed up a few paces and away from Paul's ire. "I'm gonna take a shower." He stated flatly moving past Holly and into another room slamming the door behind him. Holly turned her attention back to the table and grabbed a large bag of sour cream and onion potato chips. Tearing the top off she happily began eating one after the other while looking over the rest of the groceries. Holly was starving and she honestly could not remember when the last time was that she had eaten. The potato chips tasted like heaven! As Holly continued to pick her way through the goodies, out of the corner of her eye she spotted a telephone! Holly's feet seemed glued to the floor and her stomach flipped with the realization that she could actually call someone. She crept quietly over to the bathroom door and pressed her ear against it; listening intently. Deciding that Paul was still showering, she padded quickly back to the kitchen. But what if Paul were to end his shower quickly and catch her placing a call? Holly decided that she needed more food first and then she would make her plan to call Mileena. First though, she would put away the mess of groceries and hopefully set a decent table for them to have some dinner.

While Holly went about her task, and in a town not far away, Paul's apartment suddenly heaved and then exploded in an ear-shattering blast. Large chunks of bricks, glass and the residence's contents scattered its debris for blocks around. Ian sat cautiously in his car several blocks away, and watched the blaze engulf everything Paul held near and dear.

Paul emerged from the bathroom feeling somewhat refreshed then noticed that Holly had set them a proper table and had put away the groceries that he had just flung around the kitchen.

She sat at the table sipping a glass of wine. "This is good!" She exclaimed holding up the glass and smiling at him sheepishly. "I just grabbed whatever." Paul grumbled as he neared the table. A cold open beer was on his side of the table and Holly had set out all the goodies Paul bought. Bowls of chips and dips, and meat and cheese sandwiches were arranged on paper plates. Paul's resolve was melting once again as he realized he too was famished. Grabbing his beer he sat down and began taking long gulps of the ice cold brew. Holly watched as he grabbed two halves of the sandwiches and shoved them wildly into his mouth.. "Thanks." He stated after eating another two halves and beginning to feel more like himself. "Just keep drinking your beers." Holly thought taking another small sip of her wine. She would not be held prisoner in this God forsaken apartment, and in this God forsaken city for long. She needed desperately to talk to Mileena. And she also wondered with a sickened heart what had happened to Mark. Holly never had a chance to say goodbye to him. And here she sat now looking at Ian's right hand man and sharing a meal and some drinks with a common thug. Paul may not have been directly responsible for killing Mark, but Holly knew that she was probably Paul's original target to begin with. She would never trust him. Ever. "I'm gonna take this in there." Paul stated taking his beer into the living room and sitting heavily upon the couch. He threw his feet upon the coffee table and leaned his head back against the couch. Holly tensed as she knew that he would be asleep soon and that she may have a chance to use that telephone that she saw earlier. She would have to be very patient though. Though every inch of her was screaming out in anxious restlessness.

"I think one of those windows will actually open." Paul muttered without looking Holly's way. "If I seem to remember correctly the one's to the right have been opened before." Holly stood awkwardly and walked over to the windows. Sure enough. The one's to the right were not sealed with old paint. You could actually see the deep crease below the window and around the frame. Holly yanked up hard and the window flew open. Cool but sticky air wafted in as Holly stood in front of it and allowed the air to cool her body. "Be careful." Paul warned. "This building doesn't have fire escapes on this side." Holly stuck her head timidly out the window and noticed that none of the floors had a means of escape. All of a sudden and from out of nowhere several fire trucks roared by below her; their sirens screaming in the late morning air. Holly backed quickly away from the window. The reverberation from the trucks bounced off the adjacent buildings doubling the sound of the blaring sirens. Holly blocked her ears with her hands until they passed by. She turned then to see Paul's reaction to the sudden blast but found him fast asleep. She watched his chest rise and fall and knew that in several minutes she would be talking to her sister.

Obscure Destination

Holly waited for almost a half an hour before she could muster the courage to use the phone without Paul hearing her. He was snoring loudly now and Holly figured that he was deeply asleep. To be certain she crept slowly over to an old television set and clicked it on; all the while watching Paul. Slowly she began turning the volume knob up higher and higher until the audio was quite loud even to Holly. She knew then that Paul would not hear her talking to Mileena if indeed he did not wake from the loud programming, nor from the fire trucks that continued to stream along the streets below her. Leaving the television volume up, Holly walked slowly backwards into the kitchen and stopped just next to the phone on the wall. Steadily reaching up, Holly slowly removed the receiver from the cradle and placed it to her ear. Sliding down the wall she landed gingerly upon her butt on the floor by the kitchen. Upon hearing the blessed dial tone, Holly's heart quickened and she broke out into a mild sweat.

Never taking her eyes off Paul and as she watched him sleep on peacefully, Holly placed the call.

"Are you positive that is where they are?" Ian barked into his cell phone. Finding out that Paul and Holly were not at Paul's apartment when it had exploded, infuriated Ian. But he was close to them now and he knew it, and this was just the confirmation Ian would need to finally finish his job. "Yea, yea! I saw Paul go into the building this morning boss; carrying bags of stuff!" The caller hollered back. "Even saw the girl lookin' out the window a couple a times." Ian tossed his phone aside, started his car, and then drove off like a shot into morning traffic.

"Holly?!?" Mileena blurted out gripping the phone in her hand and listening to her sister talking a million miles a minute. "My God where are you!?"

"I've been so worried about you and so much has happened since the last time we talked!" She relayed almost hysterical. Some things Holly said Mileena was able to understand, and some things were lost, as Holly's voice was barely above a whisper. "Shhhhh Mileena don't talk!" Holly instructed as she kept an unmoving eye on Paul. "I need you to go right now and book me a flight from New York's La Guardia airport to Detroit Metro and have it waiting for me at the departures desk." Holly was shivering from head to toe as if it were only thirty degrees in the darkened apartment. She knew that it was only a matter of minutes before Paul began to wake up from his nap. "Where are you Holly?" Mileena repeated as she wrote down Holly's instructions quickly. "Mil I don't know! In New York somewhere!" Holly breathed exasperated. "My guess is not too far from the airport. I fell asleep in the car though." She relayed pensively. "Please just do this now Mileena." Holly begged as Paul suddenly stirred and shifted his position on the couch. Holly flinched and immediately hung up the phone then quickly took her spot back at the kitchen table fighting against a rapidly approaching anxiety attack. Now all Holly had to do was get out of this apartment and find her way to the airport. Surely that wouldn't be a difficult task. She had always heard about the generosity of New Yorkers and she was certain that someone would come to her aid. Glancing around the apartment she spied her purse sitting on the end table next to the couch. Shaking and rising slowly, Holly padded quietly over to the table and cautiously lifted her bag into her arms.

Heading to the door quickly, Holly stole one last glance behind her and noticed Paul had not moved a muscle. Gingerly she took the doorknob in her hand and threw open the door. Holly ran then. As fast as her legs would take her and to the stairwell that would lead her down six floors to entrance of the building and out to the street. "Hey! Stop!" A man's voice yelled as she passed an apartment with an open door. Holly jumped slightly sideways coming in contact with the hall wall. Her steps slowed slightly as she reached the stairs, and then she bounded down them two at a time. "Paul!" The man's voice yelled from somewhere behind her. "She's runnin'!"

Paul bolted awake and shook his head violently. He thought that he heard yelling and upon opening his eyes and looking around quickly he noticed the front door standing wide open. "Paul!" The man hollered again as he reached the apartment and looked inside. "Come on man. She's heading downstairs and if she hits the streets we're in trouble." Paul leapt to his feet and grabbed his jacket. The two men tore out of the apartment and down the hallway that lead to the stairs.

Ian's car swerved in and out of traffic as he drove frantically through the heavy city traffic. He only had a few more blocks to drive and he would be sitting in front of the apartment building now occupied by Holly and Paul. He had very reliable information confirming this. The informant also knew that if he even dared to think about conning Ian, he would be as dead as the couple he was after. Ian's handgun was fully loaded and sitting on the seat next to him. He would not miss either of them this time.

By the time Holly reached the bottom floor and was into the lobby area of the building she could hear Paul and the other man hollering after her, and lumbering quickly down the stairs behind her. She needed to get out of this building and to a safe hiding place quickly. Holly noticed that when she was back at the apartment and looking out the window, that directly across the street and to the right of their building was a coffee shop and a liquor store on opposite corners. She chose the coffee shop. Holly practically leapt out the front door and onto the sidewalk; moving quickly in the direction of the coffee shop. She was then inundated with such a pitch of clamor the likes of which she had never experienced before. Hordes of people seemed to swoop down from every direction then; enveloping her in a human blanket. Every inch of space around her seemed to be flooded with sounds; rumbling engines, blaring horns, shrill whistles, and voices both pleasant and enraged. It was utter chaos to Holly and she had to stop and get her bearings before proceeding. Holly noticed a large mob of people moving quickly across the busy thoroughfare. She ran up to the crowd and mocked their pace as they crossed the street. She was feeling dizzy and much out of sorts in this mass of people and it seemed as though several people were glaring in her direction; somehow knowing that she was not of their kind. Holly could just imagine how she looked. It had been at least a day since she showered or even applied any makeup. Her long, unruly hair laid heavy against her back. Once across the street she darted quickly into the coffee shop and ran full speed up to the counter. A middle-aged woman was busy pouring coffee behind the counter and winced slightly as she saw Holly near her. "Please." Holly began out of breath. "Can you help me?"

Paul and his partner reached the bottom floor and saw no signs of Holly. "Damnit!" Paul roared. "You were supposed to keep an eye on the apartment!" His yells echoing off the lobby's walls. The two men bounded through the front door together and into the throng of mid afternoon activity. Holly was nowhere in sight. Paul's eyes darted everywhere. She wouldn't get far. Holly was green to the city streets and it would only be a matter of time before Paul could locate her and get her safely back to the apartment and out of Ian's radar. "Let's try the liquor store over there." The man suggested.

Ian's car flew around the final corner of his destination nearly missing a mass transit bus as it headed to its next stop. The buss's horn suddenly blared loudly behind Ian. "Screw you asshole!" Ian yelled flipping the driver the bird. Unexpectedly, and right in Ian's sight, was Paul running across the street with another man. "You can't hide from me forever you son of a bitch." Ian stated flatly as he stomped on the gas and directed his car right for the two men.

"Honey slow down and tell me what's going on!" The waitress replied as she directed Holly behind the lunch counter. "Here, have a glass of water." She offered as she watched Holly take the glass and immediately gulp down the entire contents . The waitress also took stock of the interior of her coffee shop the store front. "I've been kidnapped!" Holly choked. "And I just escaped that apartment building across the street. But now there are two men after me!" She cried taking another gulp of water. The waitress suddenly spied out of the corner of her eye two men bounding across the street heading for the liquor store. And then simultaneously the two women heard the sound of breaks screeching. Holly's head shot up and she saw two men leaping away from a careening car. She blinked quickly not believing her eyes. It was Ian! He was driving madly threw the crowd of people outside of the coffee shop and trying to run over Paul and the other man. "Oh my God Paul!" Holly yelled as she ran towards the front door. "Wait! Don't go out there!" The waitress screamed.

As Paul and his partner neared the other side of the street he noticed several people yelling and scrambling to get out of the way of a black sedan that was coming fast and furious through the crowd. Utterly amazed, Paul noticed that Ian was behind the wheel and heading straight for them. As Paul dove swiftly out of the way, Ian's car nearly missed Paul's lower body as it flew by him. Paul landed hard on his side upon the pavement and looked up to see his partner's body flying through the air. His body came to rest upon the sidewalk and lay motionless. Ian's sedan continued on its path as it careened out of control and smashed head on into the liquor store's front windows. Out of the blue, Paul heard Holly screaming for him from somewhere in the crowd. "Holly get down!" He roared catching sight of Holly running across the street towards him. All of a sudden Ian's sedan abruptly exploded into flames and Paul saw Ian running from the burning vehicle and then duck down behind several newspaper boxes. He winced as he got hastily to his feet and ran towards Holly. "Get down! Get down!" Paul screamed as he began to feel the effects of bullets entering his body. The pain was like a searing fire splitting apart his skin.

Holly screamed as she saw Paul being picked apart by bullets. Pieces of his clothes sprang off his body and blood ran fluidly down his chest, arms and legs. She knew that Ian had escaped the inferno of his car and was hidden out of sight. She also knew that Ian was killing Paul.

For Paul had betrayed Ian, and Ian was making him pay with his life. Paul wobbled, tripped, stumbled, and fell to his knees as he tried to make his way to Holly; valiantly flailing his arms about and shouting for her to get down. Holly was awash with horror and panic and her mind reeled as she stood in the middle of the street viewing the pandemonium happening all around her. Suddenly Holly's shoulder rocketed back and sheer torture enveloped her bicep. Crying out, Holly seized her shoulder with her hand and turned to run from the mayhem. She ran wildly passed the crowd of people who had amassed on the corners and filled the streets. She had to get to the airport. Mileena was sending her a ticket to come home. She would be fine once she got home. Hot, bitter tears streamed down her face as Holly sobbed feeling almost childlike. Little girl lost. Several more gunshots rang out behind her and Holly could here them pinging off trash cans and breaking through windows around her. Two more shots pealed off and then silence. An array of sirens shrieked behind her as Holly ran on, not sure of her whereabouts. Her arm pulsed with a pain that she had never experienced before. She glanced quickly to the wound and noticed that it was a deep gash and not a bullet imbedded into her shoulder. Holly's vision began blurring and her head was swimming with thoughts of the past and the present. She saw Mileena helping her move into her apartment in Michigan. She saw Mark dressed for their wedding as she tried to help him with his tie. She just had to make it home. And as Holly ran deeper and deeper into the unfamiliar city streets she never knew that Ian, the last person who was a threat to her life, lay dead in the streets behind her.

Epilogue

Mileena paced anxiously back and forth. Her bright blue eyes darted quickly all around the very busy airport terminal. Throngs of people milled about and the energy level was very high; matching Mileena's heightened emotional state. It had been over twenty-four hours since she had spoken to Holly on the phone and had received very hasty directions for Mileena to book a flight from La Guardia airport to Detroit Metro, and to also have the ticket waiting at the departures desk for her when she arrived. Mileena made the decision then and there that she would meet her sister in New York City to make certain that Holly made it all the way home safely. Mileena had no way of telling when Holly would be arriving, nor did she know just where in this enormous city Holly was. But she knew in her heart that she would not return home without her sister. From what Mileena could gather from the last two phone calls from Holly, Trevor Morgan's brother Ian had come to Michigan from New York City to exact his revenge on Holly for the death of his brother. He had also brought with him his right hand man Paul Murphy; who was under the guise of the High School principle at Holly's school. Somewhere along the way, Holly, Paul and Ian came to New York City. And Holly and Paul were then held up in an apartment somewhere in the city. Mileena had no clue where Ian was. Holly's final call had been hushed and erratic as Holly indicated to Mileena that she was going to escape that apartment and head immediately to the airport. But that was many hours ago and Mileena was beside herself with worry. Holly had never been to a city as large as New York City and the thought of her sister all alone in a strange place made Mileena's stomach turn.

"Mileena please sit down. We can do nothing right now but wait until Holly arrives here at the airport. We have an all points bulletin out with the all the local police departments here, so either way she will find us or we will find her." Mark indicated as he stood slowly and winced against his bandaged wounds.

Printed in the United States
70663LV00001B/22-30

9 781425 977566